"A marvelous read!"

Rodney Stark, codirector, Institute for Studies of Religion, Baylor University

"Jim Papandrea has done it again. An eminent scholar and theologian of the church fathers who has also written about Christianity in popular cinema, blends his love of history with his passion for narrative tales. This unique work punctuates a wonderful fictional story with pithy lessons about the life of early Christians. Dr. Papandrea's style makes this a great read for anyone from age 12 to 112. Bravo!"

Anthony Gill, author of *The Political Origins of Religious Liberty*

"James L. Papandrea's imaginative narrative builds on a substantial amount of strong historical scholarship, yet it is presented in a fresh and unique way. Contemporary readers will sense both continuity and discontinuity between the earliest church and their own lives. When looking back at first century Christians in Rome, current practices of the faith amid modern cultural challenges appear both familiar and strange at the same time. One does not need to agree with every aspect of Papandrea's imaginative narrative to benefit greatly from his historical re-creation. I occasionally teach a course in Rome and this is now a required textbook; any Christian visiting this great city should read this book before they go!"

Kelly M. Kapic, professor of theological studies, Covenant College

A WEEK IN THE LIFE OF ROME

◆

JAMES L. PAPANDREA

IVP Academic

An imprint of InterVarsity Press
Downers Grove, Illinois

InterVarsity Press
P.O. Box 1400, Downers Grove, IL 60515-1426
ivpress.com
email@ivpress.com

InterVarsity Press® is the book-publishing division of InterVarsity Christian Fellowship/USA®, a movement of students and faculty active on campus at hundreds of universities, colleges, and schools of nursing in the United States of America, and a member movement of the International Fellowship of Evangelical Students. For information about local and regional activities, visit intervarsity.org.

All Scripture quotations, unless otherwise indicated, are the author's translation.

All interior photos are by James L. Papandrea.

Cover design: Bradley Joiner
Interior design: Beth McGill

Images: © Peter Zelei Images / Getty Images

ISBN 978-0-8308-2482-3 (print)
ISBN 978-0-8308-7261-9 (digital)

Printed in the United States of America ♾

InterVarsity Press is committed to ecological stewardship and to the conservation of natural resources in all our operations. This book was printed using sustainably sourced paper.

Library of Congress Cataloging-in-Publication Data
A catalog record for this book is available from the Library of Congress.

P	20	19	18	17	16	15	14	13	12	11	10	9	8	7	6	5	4	3	2	1
Y	35	34	33	32	31	30	29	28	27	26	25	24	23	22	21	20	19			

THIS BOOK ABOUT THE PAST
IS DEDICATED TO THE FUTURE:

To my birthday buddy,
Julia

To my confirmation sponsee,
Evan

To our godson,
Jackson

And to our nieces and nephews,
Paige, Spencer, Claire,
and Daltin

◆◇◆

CONTENTS

Acknowledgments

I AM ONE OF THOSE PEOPLE who think out loud, trying out ideas as I hear them come out of my mouth. That means that my trusted colleagues and my closest friends are often the unfortunate ones who have to hear the untested theories and half-baked ideas that will never get published. I want to thank them for their patience and for their honest feedback in conversation. In terms of the present book, I especially want to thank some of those colleagues who are also friends, including Mike Aquilina, Charlie Cosgrove, and Stephanie VanSlyke. Your feedback and conversations about this book were very much appreciated. I also want to thank Dan Reid and everyone at InterVarsity Press for making me feel welcome in the IVP family.

The Main Characters

Stachys—A Greek freedman, about forty-five years old. Formerly a slave in the household of Urbanus, he is now a client of Urbanus and a businessman. As a freedman of a Roman citizen, he has citizenship. Recently "married" to Maria (though they do not have a legally registered marriage), he is the stepfather of Marcus. He has a twelve-year-old son from a previous marriage, named Tertius, whose mother died in childbirth when Tertius was only a year old. About seven years after our story, Stachys will be greeted by the apostle Paul when he writes his letter to the Roman Christians, in Romans 16:9.

Maria—A formerly wealthy Jewish widow from Jerusalem, who supported the ministry of Jesus and the apostles. After James was martyred, when Peter escaped from prison, she spent the last of her fortune smuggling Peter out of Jerusalem, bringing him to Rome in the year AD 42, along with her son, Marcus, and her servant, Rhoda. She married the widower Stachys just before the Jews were expelled from Rome by the Emperor Claudius, which meant that she and Rhoda could stay in Rome. Maria is known to the church as Mary of Jerusalem (Acts 12:12).

Tertius—Stachys's twelve-year-old son and Maria's stepson. His mother died in childbirth when he was only a year old. When Tertius is older, he will work as a scribe for the apostle Paul and will take Paul's dictation for the letter to the Romans. He will take that opportunity to greet those of his home church in Romans 16:22.

Marcus—Maria's son and Stachys's stepson, he is twenty-eight years old. Cousin to the apostle Barnabas and associate of the apostle Paul, Marcus is also known as John Mark and was a traveling companion of Paul and Barnabas on their first missionary journey (Acts 15:37-39; Col 4:10; Philem 24). Marcus had returned to Rome to bring his mother out of the city following the edict of Claudius, but he arrived to find that his mother had married Stachys. Now he is leading the house church that meets in Stachys's home as well as leading the whole church of Rome as they await the return of the apostle Peter from the Jerusalem Council. He is also working on writing his Gospel.

Urbanus—A wealthy Roman landowner and merchant of the equestrian class. He is the patron of his former slave Stachys. He is in his mid-fifties, and he is more than twenty years older than his wife. He and his wife, Sabina, have two daughters, Tryphaena and Tryphosa. He will be greeted by the apostle Paul when he writes his letter to the Roman Christians, in Romans 16:9.

Sabina—The wife of Urbanus, from a wealthy family of the senate class. Mother of Tryphaena and Tryphosa. She is about thirty years old.

Rhoda—A Jewish freedwoman, formerly a servant in the Jerusalem household of Maria (Acts 12:13). No one is sure exactly how old she is.

Philologus—A free, but poor, Roman. He does not have citizenship because he is a "foreigner," from outside Italy. He is one of the deacons in the church of Rome and is in his late twenties. Philologus and Julia have five children: Prima, Olympas, twins Nereus and Nerea, and Anastasia. Philologus, Julia, and three of their children will be greeted by the apostle Paul when he writes his letter to the Roman Christians, in Romans 16:15.

Julia—Philologus's common-law wife. She was "married" to Philologus at age twelve, though they do not have a registered marriage. She is nineteen years old and has five children, which is unusual—not that she had so many children in so short a time but that all five of them have survived. Julia, her husband, Philologus, and three of their children will be greeted by the apostle Paul when he writes his letter to the Roman Christians, in Romans 16:15.

Scrap—An eight-year-old slave boy in the household of the senator Titus Flavius Clemens the Elder. He will take his master's name when he is freed and will eventually be known to the church as Clement, bishop of Rome.

Clemens the Younger—The son of Titus Flavius Clemens the Elder and a deacon in the church of Rome. He will later be called Clement when he is mentioned by Paul in Philippians 4:3.

Prisca—The daughter of Aquila and Priscilla. When they left Rome, she stayed behind to manage their awning shop. There was at one time a gathering of Jewish Christians who met in their shop, but that gathering is no longer meeting since the edict of Claudius banished Jews from Rome. The name Prisca is a shortened version of Priscilla, so references to Prisca in the letters of Paul are actually references to her mother, Priscilla.

Pudens—A senator of Rome who is a Christian. He is mentioned in 2 Timothy 4:21. According to tradition, the apostle Peter made Pudens's home the headquarters for his ministry in Rome. Pudens has two daughters, Pudenziana and Prassede.

Lucius Geta—Prefect of the Praetorian Guard, which is the elite bodyguard of the emperor. The praetorians were very powerful in Rome. They had organized the assassination of the previous emperor, Caligula, and had put the present emperor, Claudius, on the throne. As prefect, Geta would have the ear of the emperor.

Narcissus—One of the emperor Claudius's most trusted freedmen. He was the emperor's personal secretary, which meant that he had the power to grant favors and even advise the emperor on important appointments. He had Claudius's third wife killed so that Agrippina, the mother of Nero, could take her place. Some of the slaves in Narcissus's household were Christians.

Linus (Aquilinus)—A leader or "shepherd" of one of the house churches in Rome. He presides over worship in a butcher's apartment. After Peter's martyrdom, Linus will become Peter's first successor as the leader of the church in Rome. He will serve as bishop of Rome from the death of Peter until AD 76.

Cletus (Anacletus)—Another shepherd of one of the house churches in Rome, he presides over the liturgy in the home of senator Pudens. He will succeed Linus as bishop of Rome from AD 76 to 88.

Apelles—The shepherd of the house church that meets in his own apartment in Trans-Tiber, the poor neighborhood across the river. He will be greeted by the apostle Paul when he writes his letter to the Roman Christians, in Romans 16:10.

Ampliatus—One of the deacons of the church in Rome. He will be greeted by the apostle Paul when he writes his letter to the Roman Christians, in Romans 16:8.

The year is AD 50. The apostles have just finished their meeting in Jerusalem, and the Christians of Rome await Peter's return . . .

1

THE DAY OF THE MOON

THE NIGHT SKY BLENDED INTO THE SEA, with no horizon and no light to be seen anywhere. The water was as dark as the bottomless pit of Tartarus, swirling and coughing, spitting and slamming itself against the hull, threatening to swallow the ship whole. Rain poured down in relentless sheets, cold and piercing through cloaks and tunics, right to the skin and bone. The ship lurched under the punishment of the waves, sweeping the feet out from under sailors and passengers alike, sending flailing arms groping toward the nearest rail. One passenger, who was leaning over the side only a moment ago, was suddenly no longer there. His screams were quickly stifled by the sound of the storm and the waves, and his fellow passengers could only look on, horrified and helpless, grasping and gripping whatever they could to hold on for their lives. Peter said a short prayer for the poor man's soul, and then closed his eyes as he tried to keep his last meal down. A flash of lightning lit up the whole ship like a curtain torn open to the daylight, and then there was the roar and echoing boom of the thunder, and it was dark again.

. . .

Stachys woke up with a start and quickly looked around to see whether anyone was there to witness the embarrassing fact that he had nodded off in his patron's atrium. He breathed a sigh of relief when he saw that he was alone. A summer breeze blew through the atrium, warm and humid, and the linen awning over the skylight rippled gently. Stachys was grateful that the awning kept the sun out of his eyes. He looked down at his tanned hands, resting on the folds of the formal toga his patron had given him. Soon, Stachys's lanky Greek limbs became uncomfortable swimming in the sea of white wool, and his hands became nervous, so he occupied them by running his fingers through his blond, curly hair and scratching his head.

"Stachys, my friend!" Urbanus entered the atrium and walked quickly over to Stachys, gripping his arm warmly. Urbanus was a large man for a Roman and could almost look Stachys in the eye. He had a mop of dark hair on his head that was once cut to match the emperor's hairstyle but had gone way past the time for another haircut. Urbanus smiled, genuinely glad to see Stachys, as his face lit up under his bushy, black eyebrows.

Stachys stood up tall, proud to be greeted so warmly by his patron. Muscular and athletic, he would have looked like a Greek statue, if not for the sun, now in his eyes, coming through the atrium skylight. He blinked with humility. "*Domin*—um, *Salve*. I trust you are well. And your noble wife, Sabina, and your daughters."

"Yes, yes, same as yesterday. Stachys, what are you doing here all by yourself?" Urbanus made a mocking frown. "I thought you had neglected to come pay your respects today. Why didn't you visit me in your turn? It's not like you to be late."

"Well, the truth is, I wasn't late. I've been here all morning, but I let the others go ahead of me."

Urbanus made another face, an exaggerated look of confusion. "What? Why would you humiliate yourself like that,

THE PATRON-CLIENT SYSTEM

Roman society functioned as a network of relationships, and some of the most important relationships were those between people who were not equals. Virtually everyone in Roman culture had a patron, a person or organization who was more wealthy and powerful, who could help out in times of need. Since life in Rome was precarious at best, and the economy of the empire was in a constant downward spiral, people needed a safety net, and that came in the form of a patron. For many people in the middle and upper classes, a man, or the head of a household, would be a client to a wealthier patron. The patron provided some measure of security and would help if the client ran into legal trouble. He would also provide gifts and occasional invitations to dinner, and sometimes even daily baskets of food or coins. In return, clients would pay their respects to the patron each morning and also provide political and moral support in the courts and when it came to voting.

Freedmen were automatically considered the clients of their former masters, and many of them even continued to live within the household. Most freed slaves in Rome continued at least some kind of relationship with their former owners.

Working-class people, who may not have had a personal patron, had their guilds. The guild functioned as a kind of fraternity, and many of these clubs did have wealthy patrons who took some responsibility for the membership. Funeral clubs made sure that a person without means would receive a decent burial when the time came. The very poor and immigrants might not have had a patron, which meant that they were always on the verge of destitution.

The emperor was considered the patron of the whole empire.

letting my other clients of lower status go ahead of you? And after they probably fought and jockeyed for position among themselves, arguing over petty differences in their net worth just to see who would be first to grovel at my feet?"

"I wanted to ask a favor, but one that I didn't want the others to hear." Stachys grew nervous, not really knowing how to say what he had come to say.

"Go on." Urbanus's tone was amiable.

"It's too much to ask, really. It's just that . . ."

"Spit it out, Stachys. I have to go to court today, and you and the others have to be there to cheer for my lawyer."

"Yes, well, the thing is . . . and I know this is not my place, but I came to ask if I might be allowed to call you by your name. I mean, instead of calling you *Dominus*."

Urbanus hesitated at first. "Have we come so far? You do remember that you were once my slave?"

"Yes, *Dom*—"

"Tell me why."

Stachys took a deep breath and scratched his head. "You know that I've joined the school of the Way-followers?"

"Yes, though you still haven't told me what a Way-follower is." Urbanus's tone was shifting from warm to annoyed.

"A Way-follower is no different from any other Roman in many ways. They are not from a particular country, and they don't even all speak the same language or have all the same customs in common. They believe much of the religion of the Judeans, but the table is open to anyone who is willing to take up their lifestyle and be initiated by baptism. They are, however, especially devoted to one particular Judean. His name was Iesua. He said that he is the *way*, and the truth, and the life."

"Wait, is this that Chrestus who was the cause of all the trouble across the river that led to the emperor banishing all the Judeans?"

"Well, they call him the *Christos*, but yes. But it wasn't his fault, or the fault of the Way-followers. But you see, for the Way-followers, Iesua the Christos is *Dominus*, he is their Lord, and they are not allowed to have any other Lord; and if I am initiated and join their table, then I am not supposed to call anyone else *Dominus*."

Now Urbanus was a little angry. "What? But I am your patron! I *am* your lord! And after my father died, I gave you your freedom so you could live with your son's mother—may the spirits bless her in Elysium. I took you from managing my olive groves to having your own olive oil business, *and* you owe me a lot of money."

"Yes, and I will always be grateful, and you will always be my patron. I would never betray you. Iesua does not ask us to abandon our patrons or dishonor them in any way. But my new wife, Maria, is very . . . insistent that I learn the rules of their cult and join their table."

Urbanus looked Stachys up and down. "You were always a good and loyal slave—and for the last fifteen years you've been a good and loyal client. I know you mean no dishonor. Hades! You were willing to completely humiliate yourself in front of all my other clients just to save me the embarrassment of having to publicly consider this question of how to address me. Tell me, Stachys, why is it that your honor has increased in my eyes simply because you are willing to be shamed in order to practice your new religion?" Before Stachys could think of an answer, Urbanus concluded, "All right. From now on, you may call me by my name, and in the mornings you will visit me first, before all my other clients."

Then Stachys found himself being pushed toward the door by Urbanus, whose arm was now around his shoulders. Urbanus went right on talking. "Now, we have to get moving because I am due in court. You and the others will meet me on the steps of the new court building, the Basilica Julia. We're due there at the third hour, so whatever you have to do now, be sure you're not

TIMES AND SEASONS

For many Romans the workday was only about six hours long. The exception would have been those businesses that stayed open during the "siesta" time, and although there seems to have been a universal assumption that everyone should have the time to go to the baths in the afternoon (including slaves), clearly the workers in the baths would have been one group of people who had a longer workday. Another group would have been shopkeepers and tavern workers, who hoped to profit from the leisure time of others. On the other hand, some sources indicate that even the shops closed up by about 1 p.m. so the shopkeepers could go to the baths. In any case, it is clear that most men in the upper classes tried to get their business done before lunch, leaving the afternoon for leisure. Most Romans, however, whether working-class men or women who maintained a home, would probably not have had the flexibility to end their workday at a scheduled time.

It's important to remember that the Romans did not have minute divisions of the hours. They marked their time by sundials and water clocks (the wealthy actually had pocket sundials). This means that keeping an appointment to the minute was not a possibility. A person might try to arrive at the beginning of the third hour, for example, but there was no way to say for sure whether it was the top of the hour, unless perhaps the meeting place was the water clock. For the most part, people who agreed to meet at a certain hour were probably used to waiting around a lot. Also, since the length of the day changed with the seasons, the length of each hour within the day would not have been consistent and could never have been more than approximate.

Therefore the typical Roman workday might have looked something like this:

Predawn: Wake, dress, and eat a minimal breakfast of bread and water

First hour (6–7 a.m.): Workday begins, school begins for children

Second hour (7–8 a.m.): Clients visit patrons

Third hour (8–9 a.m.): Business in the forum begins, the courts are open

Fourth hour (9–10 a.m.): Work/business day continues

Fifth hour (10–11 a.m.): Business day ends for upper-class Romans

Sixth hour (11 a.m.–noon): Shopping and/or lunch

Seventh hour (Noon–1 p.m.): Lunch and/or going to the baths

Eighth hour (1–2 p.m.): Going to the baths, leisure time for the wealthy

Ninth hour (2–3 p.m.): People going out to dinner are getting ready

Tenth hour (3–4 p.m.): The wealthy gather for dinner

Eleventh hour (4–5 p.m.): Dinner

Twelfth hour: (5–6 p.m.): Dinner (normal dinner lasted two hours, more for a banquet)

The day ended at sundown, and most people stayed indoors after that.

The Roman calendar was based on the zodiac and marked with lucky and unlucky days. Important days of the month included the first of the month, called the Calends, as well as the Nones (the seventh of the month in March, May, July, and October; the fifth in the rest of the months) and the Ides (the fifteenth of the month in March, May, July, and October; the thirteenth in the rest of the months). The Senate met on the Calends and the Ides every month except September and October, when it was on hiatus.

late. I need all the support I can get. Oh, almost forgot." Urbanus pulled a small leather bag from the fold in his toga and took out a silver *denarius*. "Here you go. So much easier than when we used to have to give out food baskets to all the clients."

"Yes, but I can tell you the clients do miss the days when the daily gift might be an invitation to dinner."

"Ha! Parasites, the lot of them." Urbanus put his arm around Stachys again. "But now that we are truly friends, you can look forward to an invitation to dinner in the near future, I promise."

Stachys left the atrium and exited Urbanus's house through a door that led out toward the Tiburtinian Road. He loved walking through the wealthy neighborhood that was outside the wall to the east of the city. He loved it because wealthy meant quiet. And since he knew that he had already missed most of the Way-followers' morning prayer gathering going on at his house, there was no need to hurry.

The Roman sun was getting hot as Stachys walked into town. There was no shade, so as much as he enjoyed the walk and the quiet, he was looking forward to the shade of the apartment buildings and the awnings in the city. He walked over the Esquiline Hill, past the potsherd dump, around the slave cemetery, and through the neighborhood of the paint sellers, entered the city proper at the Esquiline Gate, and then down into the city and toward the Three Fora.

Once inside the city gate, the streets became narrow, winding, and muddy. He laughed at himself for wishing for the shade of the narrow streets and forgetting about how they were so filled with mud and dung that it was impossible to tell the difference between the two. He pulled up on the bottom of his toga and did his best to keep it out of the mud and *merda*.

The closer he got to the center of the city, the more the streets became clogged with merchants yelling out their wares, prostitutes standing in the doorways and arches, taverns overflowing their thresholds, teachers trying to keep the attention of their students by shouting their lectures, fortunetellers and potion sellers calling out their promises, and barbers shaving and cutting hair. It was as if for a few hours each day Rome became one big shop. Stachys pushed through the crowd until finally he was able step into a more open space at the Forum of Augustus. He took a right turn at the Temple of Mars. As he looked into the sky he could see gray clouds on the horizon, and he wondered whether rain was coming.

Stachys lived near the foot of the Capitoline Hill, just outside the wall at the Fontinalis Gate, at the beginning of the Flaminian Road that led to the north. When he arrived at his house, the morning prayer meeting was just breaking up. He walked through the group of people still milling around and went to his wife, who was alternating between singing a psalm and blowing out candles.

Create in me a clean heart, O Lord, renew a right spirit in me.

Do not cast me away from your presence, do not take your Holy Spirit from me.

Stachys snuck up behind her, put his hands on her hips, and kissed her neck.

Maria startled a bit and hunched her shoulders. "Beloved." Her long, dark hair flipped to the side as she turned around and held out her hand for the denarius.

Stachys put the denarius in her hand. "Apple of my eye."

Maria's full lips curved up, and an asymmetrical smile emerged under her prominent nose. "Oh, you've been reading the Scriptures. That makes me so happy."

"Your neck is like an ivory tower. Your nose is like the tower of Lebanon."

"Don't overdo it," she said through a smirk. She handed him two bronze *sesterces* for his lunch and shave.

ROMAN COINS AND MONEY

Roman coins came in gold, silver, bronze, and copper. The gold coin, the *aureus*, was the most valuable. It was about the size of a dime and was worth twenty-five *denarii*, or one hundred *sesterces*.

The *denarius*, the silver coin, was also about the size of a dime. One *denarius* was worth four sesterces and was considered a standard day's wage for a working man, although the underemployed of Rome were living on half a *denarius* per day.

The bronze coin was the *sestertius* (plural *sestertii*, often translated *sesterces*), about the size of a silver dollar and worth one-fourth of a *denarius*. A Roman might expect to pay one *sestertius* for lunch, and for three *sesterces* he could get a room at an inn, including dinner.

The copper coin was called an *as*. Ten *asses* make a *denarius*, which is why the name of the *denarius* is related to the root for the word *ten*. However, there were apparently times when the value of the *as* fluctuated, and it could take as many as sixteen or eighteen *asses* to make a denarius.

The front of a Roman coin had the emperor's portrait, along with abbreviations for his official titles, such as IMP (short for *imperator*, meaning "emperor"); COS (for consul, along with the number of times he had held that position—this was the equivalent of putting a date on the coin); PONT MAX (for *pontifex maximus*, the official high priest of Rome); PP (for *pater patriae*, "father of the fatherland"); and other possible titles such as those derived from places the emperor had conquered. On coins issued in the year AD 95, if one were to add up the numerical value of the letters in the abbreviations of the titles of the emperor Domitian (assuming something like a = 1, b = 2, etc.), the sum would be 666 (see Rev 13:18). For more on the Roman emperors and the book of Revelation, see my book *The Wedding of the Lamb*.

On the back of the coin were personifications of the emperor's policies or images that evoked the ways in which an emperor wanted the people to think about his reign. For example, Claudius's coins proclaimed his reign as a new Augustan age with the word *libertas*.

Rome's economy was based more on taxation than production. The city of Rome especially had to import almost everything, and most of it came from the provinces. The Romans claimed that their main export was peace, which they would say was a fair trade for their colonization; however, the declining production eventually put the economy into a recession that forced future emperors to devalue the coinage by reducing the amount of precious metal in the coins. This caused people to lose faith in the currency and turn more and more to bartering, which in turn made it difficult for the Roman emperors to pay the legions. In addition, inflation was surpassing any increase in wages that a working man might hope for, to the point where it was difficult to make a living without participating in the networks of corruption that existed in the city. If a worker were honest, he or she was aware of making less money every year. Rent was also increasing, with investors renting apartments just to sublet them, so it was becoming harder and harder to find an apartment to rent where one was dealing directly with the owner of the building.

For those Romans who were wealthy enough to have a savings of cash, their money was kept in the temples. Many Roman temples had storerooms underneath them that functioned as banks. They were guarded, of course, but it seems that attempts at robbing the temple were rare, since it would have been considered sacrilegious. The temple of Saturn in the Old Forum was the imperial treasury. It held the emperor's personal money as well, since there was little, if any, distinction between the empire's money and the emperor's money. Although business was frowned on in the senate class, some equestrians made their money by making loans for interest. They were the venture capitalists of the Roman Empire.

In order to be a member of the senate class, one had to be a millionaire—literally. It took an income of at least one million sesterces per year. Four hundred thousand sesterces per year were required to join the equestrian class.

Figure 1.1. Roman gold aureus showing the portrait of Claudius (National Roman Museum, Palazzo Massimo, Rome)

Figure 1.2. Roman gold aureus showing the portrait of Agrippina. Note her title, "Augusta." (National Roman Museum, Palazzo Massimo, Rome)

Figure 1.3. The Temple of Saturn. Note the space below the façade, which was used as the storehouse for the treasury of the Roman state. (Republican Forum, Rome)

"Stachys, old man!"

Stachys turned to greet his stepson, Marcus, who was extending his meaty hand and stubby fingers for a handshake. Even though Marcus was a relatively young man, his hairline was already visibly receding. But his eyes were sharp and clear as they stared out from under his unibrow and locked onto Stachys's eyes. Stachys gripped Marcus's hand. "*Salve*, Marcus. How was the prayer gathering?"

"It was a blessing; thanks for asking." Marcus gestured toward a young woman standing nearby. "Stachys, you know Prisca, don't you? Her parents are Aquila and Priscilla, the awning makers. They left the city with the banishment of the Judeans, but since her mother is Roman, she was able to stay behind to manage their shop."

Stachys bowed his head in respect toward the young noblewoman as Maria put her hands on the shoulders of Marcus and Prisca. "Wouldn't she make a perfect wife for my Johnny?"

"Mother," Marcus interrupted, then sighed. "I'm twenty-eight years old. Please don't call me Johnny. And anyway, it's hard enough for us to keep our heads down here in Babylon without people using our Judean names. You have to call me by my baptism name, Marcus, like everyone else. And you're not Miriam, you're Maria." He turned to Prisca. "I'm sorry about that." Prisca just smiled and looked down at the floor, blushing.

Marcus raised his voice to get everyone's attention. "Now that Stachys is here, I have an announcement." Everyone became silent. "I've received a letter from Peter." The Way-followers held their breath. "By now he'll be on his way back to us." Every held breath was released with a sigh of relief and exclamations of joy. "He's coming by ship, and should be here within a few days. But because of the banishment of the Judeans, he's going to have to avoid the main port of Puteoli and come in through Ostia. We have some friends there who will meet him and get him safely off the ship under cover of night. Then we'll get him into Rome."

The group vocalized their concern. "I know it's dangerous to travel at night," Marcus said, "but we don't really have a choice. We have to smuggle him in. But there's more news. The council in Jerusalem has made a decision about non-Judean believers."

Again the assembled group held its collective breath. Marcus went on. "Non-Judean believers who want to be baptized—" He paused for effect, but his smile spoiled the surprise. "Do *not* have to follow all the laws of our ancestors. They do not have to restrict their diet, and the men do not have to be circumcised." An audible but restrained cheer rose up from the group. "They do, however, have to refrain from eating meat sacrificed to idols."

"*Va cacá!*" Philologus's face turned red when the whole group looked at him with dismay over his outburst. His wife, Julia, put her hand on his arm as if to quiet him, but her long, red hair, parted in the middle and tied like a horse's tail with colorful ribbons, only served to help draw everyone's attention to them.

Marcus frowned. "Problem, Philologus?"

Philologus avoided making eye contact with Marcus. "It's just that sometimes that's the only meat I get all year. And I really like meat." A few people laughed.

Marcus tried to suppress a smile, and it turned into a smirk. "Yeah, I get it. We all like meat. But I think the council's decision is the right one. We have to separate ourselves from idolatry, and that's one way we keep ourselves holy."

When the others finally filed out of their house, Marcus kissed his mother on the cheek and nodded toward Stachys. "I'm going to walk Prisca home."

"Wait," Maria stopped him and grabbed his arm. She could tell there was more on Marcus's mind. "What else did the letter say?"

"Well, you know, the regular stuff." Maria stared at him, and he could tell he was not getting out the door without telling her the whole story. Marcus sighed. "Reading between the lines, I got the impression that there's still some disagreement among the apostles. Between Peter and Paul mostly. Do you know they're starting to call Paul the apostle to the nations? Can you believe that? The nerve of that guy. I mean, Peter converted the first Romans, and to this day he's converted more non-Judeans than Paul by a long shot. And I know Paul, and I'm just a little concerned that he's getting too big for himself."

"And who appointed you judge over the apostles?" It was Rhoda. She had known Marcus since he was a boy, and although she was once a servant in his mother's household, she had no hesitation about putting him in his place. She raised her eyebrows under her raven-black bangs and waited for his response.

"Anyway," Marcus tried to get back to the point, "we'll know more when Peter gets here."

As soon as they were alone, Maria took Stachys's hands in hers and looked into his eyes. "Well? Did you ask him?"

Stachys smiled. "Yes, I did. And he said yes."

Maria smiled even wider. "I'm so anxious for you to join our table. Then, when you're baptized, we can have our union blessed. I would feel so much better if we could, since we couldn't have a registered marriage."

"Who cares about that?" Stachys protested. Then he lowered his voice and gestured toward Prisca as she was going out the door with Marcus. He was immediately self-conscious about his own status, since he was a freedman, just like Aquila. "Aquila and Priscilla don't have a registered marriage. Same with Philologus and Julia. But it doesn't seem to matter to them. Where are they from again?"

"But it *does* matter," Maria squeezed his hands. "Not what the Romans think. But it matters to the Lord. Aquila and Priscilla had

MARRIAGE AND THE FAMILY
IN THE ROMAN WORLD

A legal marriage, or what I am calling a "registered" marriage, was basically a contract. Think of it as a prenuptial agreement that also served to function as a marriage license (some of these contracts required the bride to promise she would not use magic on her new husband!). However, most people who did not have Roman citizenship could not have a registered marriage because they could not legally make a contract. Even people who could have a registered marriage often did not bother with it for a variety of reasons. The contract required a dowry paid by the bride's family to the groom. However, if the bride had no family, or the family had no money, the bride often would have no dowry, and in that case there would be no marriage contract. Sometimes the dowry could be paid in property, and in some cases even as little as the bride's wardrobe or jewelry could be considered a dowry for the purposes of the contract. But in the city of Rome the main reason anyone made a marriage contract was to make sure that the children who came from the registered marriage would be considered legitimate and would be able to inherit the parents' estate.

If there was no contract, couples who decided to create a family together would have the equivalent of a common-law marriage. Probably most marriages in the Roman Empire were not registered. Only a registered marriage produced legitimate children, so children from a common-law marriage were considered illegitimate. However, that didn't carry the stigma that we might think. It limited their legal options, and technically the children took their name and status from the mother's side of the family, but for most of the people in that situation, it didn't matter much. Such common-law marriages are simply called marriages in the literature, and the couples are referred to as husbands and wives. Even marriages between slaves were recognized, though in that case husbands and wives could still be sold separately, and a slave still would have been sexually available to his or her owner. (The first Christian emperor, Constantine, decreed that slave families should not be broken up by sale or transfer of property.)

There were some laws limiting who could legally marry. No one from the senate class could marry a freedperson (former slave), and a woman of the equestrian class could not marry a freedman. No freeborn person could marry a former prostitute. However, couples could and did cohabitate across social class lines, apparently without doing too much harm to their social standing. And in any case, men were always free to cohabit with a courtesan or slave, especially if they were widowed. All this is to say that the laws that restricted registered marriage did not stop people from creating unions and making families. While we read that marriages in the upper classes were often marriages of convenience that focused more on how the contract benefited the extended family than on the desires of the bride and groom, it must have been the case that many couples got together for the same reasons that people do today.

Of those who had registered marriages, many were arranged. Children as young as ten years old could be engaged, and marriage could happen as early as age twelve for girls and fourteen for boys. However, there was a two-year limit on the length of the betrothal period, so most of the time, girls were engaged around age fifteen and married in their late teens, and boys were engaged in their late teens and married around twenty, unless they went into the military. In that case they married when they got out, at around age twenty-seven, or at least by about thirty. The end result of all this was that Roman husbands and wives tended to have a greater difference in age than we're used to—often as much as ten years' difference or more for a first marriage and an even greater gap for second and third marriages.

Divorce was extremely easy and common, as much for registered as nonregistered marriages. It could be initiated by either spouse. This means that there must have been a lot of fear of abandonment on the part of women, since a woman on her own was a woman in danger. For this reason, in the event of a divorce the dowry would have to be returned so that the woman would not be destitute. This may have served as a deterrent to divorce, if the dowry was substantial. On the other hand, even husbands could be at the mercy of a networking father-in-law, who would demand the return of the dowry in order to enter into a new marriage contract. Married women were still tied to their father's family, and a woman's father could initiate a divorce in order to make a better match for his daughter. As time went by, wealthy husbands and wives increasingly kept their family's money and property separate so that parting ways would be easier.

The prevalence of second marriages and blended families was probably greater than it is today. A lower average life expectancy combined with a high rate of death during childbirth meant that many people were widowed, and women under fifty years old who found themselves widowed were expected to remarry within a time between ten months and two years. Virtually everyone in the upper classes had stepchildren. Wealthy Romans especially do not seem to have thought of marriage as a lifelong bond the way we know that Jews and Christians did. For them, marriage was a political and financial arrangement meant to benefit their extended families. Divorce and remarriage was part of the usual social climbing that Romans with money engaged in. For this reason, many Romans (especially men) had no hesitation in looking for love outside the home. Roman marriage was sexually open (at least for men), and sex with slaves and prostitutes was expected and considered normal. Divorce was rarely over infidelity, since the Roman definition of infidelity did not include sex with slaves or prostitutes. The problem with infidelity in Roman eyes was not so much the sex but rather the potential for bringing shame on one's family (and possible exile) if one were caught with the wife of a powerful man. Adultery in Roman law was limited to those situations where a woman in a registered marriage might bear illegitimate children, who would unknowingly inherit money and property from a man who was not their father. Therefore it should be no surprise that in the event of divorce, the legitimate children of a registered marriage stayed with their father.

Figure 1.4. Portrait of a Roman couple. In this fresco, found in a Roman house in Pompeii, the woman holds a wax tablet and stylus, indicating that she was educated, and the man holds a scroll, which may symbolize an administrative position in Pompeii. (National Archaeological Museum, Naples)

their union blessed by an apostle of the Lord Iesua. When Peter
returns, he can do that for us. But first you have to be baptized."

"Yes, but . . ."

"Look, if you didn't want to be with me, you could have done
what any other man would have done—you could have taken a
much younger wife, a proper Roman girl who wouldn't have had
so many of her own ideas, and her own religion, and who would
have had a dowry to give you so you could just have a regular
registered marriage."

Stachys shrugged sheepishly. "The gods gave you to me. Who
am I to argue with them?"

"The gods!" Maria scoffed. "I was not theirs to give! Did a
stone give you life? Did a painted statue give you air to breathe?"

"Well, I never said I was against it. Like I've told you before,
the dowry thing means nothing to me. I respect that you spent
all of your money to get you and your entourage to Rome. That
brings honor to your name, Judean or not. We can have this
blessing, when the time is right. But now I have to go to court."

As he walked out the door, Maria was still talking to him. "It
wasn't an entourage. They're not *my* followers. Anyway, someone
had to get Peter out of Jerusalem."

Stachys made his way through the gate and around the Capitoline Hill toward the Old Forum. The awnings of the forum
shaded him as he made his way around the senate house and
past the rostrum. There he heard Polybius, one of the emperor's
most powerful freedmen, making an announcement.

"Our illustrious father, the emperor, Tiberius *Claudius* Caesar
Augustus, has decreed and provided for three days of games, to
celebrate the occasion of the adoption of his stepson, Lucius
Domitius Ahenobarbus, who from this day forward will be known
as *Nero* Claudius Caesar. The three days of games will commence
on the third day after today. Regular work will be suspended. Men

are required to wear the toga. Furthermore, the emperor, in his generosity, has decreed that there will be a distribution of bread on the second day after today, the day preceding the first day of the games. The distribution will begin at the fourth hour in the Field of Mars. Those who wish to benefit from the distribution must appear in person. No one may receive for another."

As Stachys passed, Polybius repeated the announcement several times, to the cheers of the people who heard it. Coming to the steps of the Basilica Julia, Stachys maneuvered his way around the men playing dice and heads or tails on the court steps. Some of them were playing a board game on the marble steps, where grooves were scratched into the stone to create the game board. As Stachys came into the cooler air of the court building, he saw Urbanus standing in the middle of a growing group of clients, gesturing wildly while talking. He was wearing his best white toga, with the thin purple stripe of the equestrian class, and in between spurts of talking with his hands, he nervously played with his gold equestrian ring.

Figure 1.5. Game board carved into the marble steps of the Basilica Julia courthouse. The rules of the game are unknown, but it may have been something like mancala.

On the other side of the aisle, in full uniform and wearing a large ivory phallus on a necklace, was Lucius Geta, the prefect of the Praetorian Guard, standing with his own supporters. Urbanus was suing Geta for payment of a contract on olives. Geta claimed he had canceled the order; Urbanus said that the olives went uncollected and grew mold in the warehouse. At first the case seemed hopeless. A civil suit against a soldier was almost always a losing proposition. And the courts generally favored the testimony of witnesses who were soldiers. But Urbanus's lawyer spoke more eloquently, and Stachys and the other clients cheered more loudly (even though most of them didn't understand a word of Latin). In the end, Urbanus won the day. Now Urbanus handed each of his clients a small bonus and sent them on their way, but held Stachys back. "Join me for lunch," he said, pulling Stachys by the arm.

They walked from the Old Forum and headed to a nearby tavern on the edge of the Suburra, the neighborhood behind the Forum of Augustus. Stachys bumped into the jugs of wine hanging from chains around the doorpost. He stumbled on the threshold, then caught up to Urbanus, who had walked up to the counter.

"Drinks are on me," Urbanus said, winking at the barmaid. She handed Urbanus two mugs and a jug of wine, mixed with water—two-thirds wine, one-third water. Urbanus paid for the drinks and then ordered some food for himself: a sausage on a stick, and a piece of flatbread with olive paste. Stachys took out his bronze *sestertius*, set it on the counter, and asked for bread and cheese.

As the two men finished their first bite of lunch, Stachys raised his mug. "Congratulations on your victory in court today."

Urbanus halfheartedly raised his mug. "Thank you. But it's an uneasy victory." He took a long drink, then put down the mug thoughtfully as he spun his gold equestrian ring around his

Figure 1.6. Remains of a Roman tavern, Ostia Antica

finger. "Yes, Geta will have to pay me what he owes me, but he's been humiliated, and that means this is not over. In fact, just taking him to court was a risky insult on my part, but the fact that I won—now I wish I could forget the whole thing. I'm worried that taking him to court may cost me more than I'm going to get from him. I paid for that victory, and now I have to watch my back. Never go to court, Stachys."

"But what can he do to you?" Stachys was concerned for his patron, partly because any misfortune a patron might suffer was bound to trickle down to the clients.

Urbanus thought for a moment. "You know that I have been maneuvering to be appointed as prefect of the grain supply?"

"Yes, and may the gods—" Stachys caught himself.

"Well, Geta has his own man he's put up for the position. Now he's going to be even more determined to see me defeated. And he has a lot of powerful friends in the imperial house."

"But you have friends too, no?"

"Yes, some. But are they the right ones? Everyone seems to be afraid of Narcissus. It's a shame how things have become so upside down, senators having to grovel at the feet of former slaves. No offense."

"None taken."

"And do I think that Geta will play by the rules? No, I do not."

Urbanus expressing his fears was making Stachys feel all the more vulnerable. This made Stachys react with just enough boldness to bring up a subject he had wanted to bring up for a long time. "I was hoping to speak to you about something, since we're on the subject."

"What is it?"

"Just as you wish to advance yourself and enhance your position, to be the prefect of the grain supply, I wish to advance myself as well. Not a political office, of course, but I was thinking, I would like to expand my business into imports. And if you become prefect of the grain supply, maybe I could have a piece of the corn-import business. That would bring more security to me and my family."

"Ah," Urbanus nodded. "That makes sense. But corn, that's a tough one. Corn is almost completely controlled by the imperial house, just like papyrus. Now, with my connections, I could probably get you into importing lumber, or maybe even wine. But, Stachys, do you really want to advance yourself? It's not as though you can become an equestrian. And anyway, the senators look down on anyone engaged in business. To them, buying commodities at one price and selling them for a profit, without doing anything to increase their value, is considered dishonest. Of course, they're hypocrites, because they just have their slaves do it for them. Really, I hate to discourage you, but advancement doesn't mean more security—it means more visibility, and more visibility means more exposure to danger. Like climbing a scaffold, the higher you go, the more dangerous the fall. Wouldn't you rather just enjoy life today and not work so hard for something that may or may not come to you another day? You should be happy with the olive oil business I set up for you. My groves produce more than enough olives, and you know you have unlimited use of my olive presses as long as you buy the olives from me. What more could you want? When you move up in Rome, you become the object of envy. And a purple stripe on your toga—" He picked up the hem of his toga and waved the thin purple stripe in the air. "That's just the same as a target on your back." He opened his small leather bag and looked inside, poking around with his finger, until he found the coin he was looking for. "My good-luck charm."

Stachys nodded. He had seen it before, but he always liked it when Urbanus brought it out. It was Urbanus's most prized possession: a gold *aureus* with the image of Julius Caesar on it. It shone like brand new from all the rubbing it received from Urbanus's fingers. Urbanus didn't say anything else; he just rubbed the gold coin and then put it back into the leather pouch. Stachys waited in silence out of respect, and they quietly went back to eating their lunch. When they were finished, Urbanus slapped the crumbs off his hands and said, "And now it's time for a shave and a bath." The two men said their goodbyes, and Stachys headed for the barber as Urbanus took the barmaid by the arm and led her up the tavern's back stairs.

Stachys didn't need to wear the toga for the rest of the day, so he stopped at home to take it off. Happy to be free of the eight-foot circle of wool (and to have the use of both of his hands now that he didn't constantly need one to keep from tripping over it), he went back out in his tunic and cloak. As he was leaving his house, he met his twelve-year-old son, Tertius, coming toward it. He smiled and waited for Tertius to greet him.

"Papa!" Tertius ran to his father and was about to throw his arms around Stachys, but then composed himself and tried to act like a man.

"Tertius, my boy. How was school?"

"More Virgil."

"Good. Always remember that before there was Rome, there was Greece. We Greeks started it all."

"Yes, Father."

"Going to help the women now?"

"Yes."

"Good. Do what Rhoda says. And be good to your stepmother!"

"I am. I mean, I will." Tertius ran into the open arms of Maria, who was waiting for him in the doorway. Although Maria was not his mother, Stachys knew she loved Tertius as though he was her own son. And since Tertius's mother died when he was so young, Maria was the only mother he ever knew. As far as he was concerned, she was the only mother he would ever need.

Stachys thought about his family. How different it had turned out from what he thought he could expect. His first wife had died giving birth, as many women did. It was not unusual, nor something to dwell on. Still, he had prayed to his gods. He had said all the right words and made the right offerings. And yet she died. And Tertius . . . his name meant "third," because he had two older brothers, neither of whom lived even to Tertius's age. A wife and two sons lost, not to mention the stillborn daughter who accompanied her mother into the underworld. Now, a new wife and stepson. And Tertius. The son of a freedman would be a citizen when he became a man, and that was something to be proud of.

Stachys got a shave and a trim, and the fact that Urbanus had paid for his drink at lunch meant that he had enough money for a manicure too. Most men liked going to the barber, sitting around on the benches, talking and playing chess. But Stachys was always conflicted as the barber cut his hair short to match the style of the emperor. It made him look like a good Roman, but he knew that his fellow Greeks called him a pretender behind his back because he had abandoned the longer hairstyle of his home country. But after all, he was a businessman, and he couldn't afford to look like a barbarian.

After his haircut, Stachys ran his fingers through his newly cut hair and made his way north on the Flaminian Road to the Baths of Agrippa, where admission was free. He knew the risk of theft was greater there, but free was free, after all, and he reasoned that there was nothing special about his clothes and shoes that anyone should want to steal them.

By the tenth hour, the Way-followers were gathering again at the home of Stachys and Maria. Marcus welcomed them and began the meeting with a prayer. After the prayer, Marcus asked whether anyone had any specific prayer requests. Julia was elbowing Philologus. Marcus teased him, "Philologus, do you want to pray for more meat?"

The group laughed, as Philologus looked down at his feet. Julia elbowed him again. Eventually, when the laughter died down, Philologus looked up. "I've been put out of my guild."

The group fell silent, and Marcus's expression changed to one of concern. "I'm sorry, Philologus. What happened?"

"I've always been able to show up late to the banquets. Get there after the sacrifice, so I don't have to take part in the idolatry. But today when I told my master-teacher that I would be late, they all ganged up on me and pressed me to make an offering to the twin gods, which I refused to do. And when I wouldn't, the stonemasons guild of the Suburra took an official vote and voted me out."

Rhoda spoke up. "Can you go to the stonemasons across the river?"

"No," Philologus answered with a sigh. "I was only a plasterer, second class. The Trans-Tiber stonemasons have their own plasterers, and anyway, I'm sure they've already sent word for them to shun me."

Everyone felt terrible, and a little uncomfortable as they could see a tear run down Julia's cheek. Thoughts of starvation, homelessness, and death—with no hope of a decent burial—ran through everyone's mind.

After a long silence, Marcus led the group in a prayer for a new job for Philologus and for the Lord to sustain Philologus, Julia, and their five children. Marcus concluded, "Lord, have mercy."

The people echoed, "Lord, have mercy."

"*Christos*, have mercy."

"*Christos,* have mercy," came the response.

"Lord, have mercy."

They all said, "Lord, have mercy."

Then Marcus took a scroll down from a shelf. "Now let's turn back to the reading of our copy of the apostle Paul's letter to the Way-followers of Thessalonica."

．　．　．

Meanwhile, on the Viminal Hill on the eastern side of the city, another group of Way-followers was gathering at the home of the senator Acilius Pudens. There his young daughters, Pudenziana and Prassede, were closing the shutters and lighting candles. Senator Pudens spoke up and got everyone's attention. "Now we should begin, so that we can be finished before dark. We don't want anyone having to walk through the Suburra after dark." He turned and nodded to a man named Cletus.

Cletus began with a prayer, which ended with the words "Lord, have mercy." Then Cletus read from a scroll a story about three men who refused to worship their emperor and the gods of the land where they were living. Instead they worshiped only the one true Deity, and for this the emperor had them thrown into a furnace to be burned alive. But their Deity saved them from the fire.

After the reading, Cletus talked about how the situation of Daniel's three friends was a lot like the situation of the Way-followers in Rome, living under an unbelieving emperor who expected them to worship his gods and betray their own. Cletus encouraged the group to do everything in their power to resist the temptation to follow the customs of the Greek and Roman religions, even if it would mean hardship or inconvenience. He ended by asking the group, "Do you confess with your mouth that Iesua is *Dominus*?"

Everyone answered, "Yes."

Cletus continued, "Do you believe in your heart that the Father raised him from the dead?"

"Yes," the group answered.

"Then you will be saved."

Then Cletus led the group in prayers for each other, for the Way-followers in other cities, and even for the emperor and the Senate.

After a blessing, the group shared a modest meal of fish and polenta, with bread, olives, and several kinds of cheese. As everyone ate, the room became silent, but soon the silence was interrupted by the arrival of an out-of-breath Philologus. He had a basket in his hand, and in the basket, wrapped in a towel, was a large piece of bread, broken from an even larger loaf. He brought the basket to Cletus, who took the bread. Then, without speaking, Philologus was out the door and gone.

Cletus held the bread in his hands and addressed the group. "Although we meet in different homes, in different parts of the city, we are one—and we are one with all Way-followers who meet in every city, in every part of the world—and so we share the one bread to remind us of our unity. Iesua said, *I am the bread of life. Your ancestors ate the manna in the wilderness, yet they died. This is the bread that comes down out of heaven, so that one may eat of it and not die. I am the living bread that came down out of heaven. If anyone eats this bread, he will live forever, and this bread that I give for the life of the world is my flesh. Truly, truly, I say to you, unless you eat the flesh of the Son of Man and drink his blood, you have no life in you. Whoever eats my flesh and drinks my blood has eternal life, and I will raise him up on the last day. For my flesh is true food, and my blood is true drink. Whoever eats my flesh and drinks my blood remains in me, and I in him.* This is the mystery of our faith. The *Christos* has died; the *Christos* is risen; the *Christos* will come again."

Cletus set the bread down on the table and lifted his eyes and hands toward the heavens. "Now let's pray the prayer that our Lord Iesua taught his disciples." Everyone joined in the Our Father, and then Cletus continued. "Brothers and sisters, John the Baptizer pointed to Iesua and said, 'Look—here is the Lamb of God, who takes away the sin of the world.' Now let's take some time to examine our spirits and ask ourselves whether we have failed to obey the commandments of the Lord." He paused for a while and then went on. "With that in mind, we confess our sins to the Lord. Lamb of God, who takes away the sins of the world, have mercy on us. Lamb of God, who takes away the sins of the world, have mercy on us. Lamb of God, who takes away the sins of the world, grant us peace." Then Cletus held the bread up for everyone to see. "Look—here is the Lamb of God, who takes away the sin of the world." He broke the bread and passed it around the room.

The gathering closed with the singing of a song—not one of the old songs of the Judeans but a new song:

Awake, O sleeper, rise up from death

And the Christos *will shine on you*

He is the risen sun, older than the morning star

His light gives life to you

2

THE DAY OF MARS

IN THE SUBURRA, behind the firewall that separated the Forum of Augustus from Rome's most notorious neighborhood, Philologus opened the wooden shutters, letting a hazy stream of light into the dark apartment. He was grateful for summer days when they didn't have to choose between letting the light in and keeping the cold out. He smiled at the wildflowers Julia had transplanted into the window boxes, and he dipped his hand into the fire bucket to pour a bit of water on them. "I hardly slept," he said to Julia. "People shouting 'Fire!' and the yelling of the fire brigade woke me up, and I couldn't get back to sleep. Third time in four days. I always feel guilty for being so happy when I realize it's not our building."

Julia smiled at him. "No need to feel guilty for being concerned about the safety of our children. Being on the fifth floor . . ." She shuddered to think of how difficult it might be to get her family out of the building if there were a fire. It made her extra careful as she warmed some stale bread over the small copper brazier.

"At least being on the fifth floor means we get light in the mornings." Philologus looked at the children. The youngest ones were already up. The twins, Nereus and Nerea, always got up together, since the first one to wake always woke the other. Anastasia, the youngest, was sitting on the end of her parents' bench bed as Julia brushed her hair. The older two were another story: Prima, the oldest, and Olympas. Philologus gave their mats a nudge with his foot. He looked at his children. "Well, I may be tired, but at least I won't have to climb any scaffolds today." He tried to sound positive, but he was wondering how he was going to feed his family. Today was a new reality for him. He had woken up with a nagging uncertainty about himself. He had no guild, which meant no work and no patron. No identity, and no way to provide.

WHERE ROMANS LIVED

Most people in Rome lived in high-rise apartment buildings called *insulae* (singular *insula*), which were built close together—with only narrow alleyways between most of them—and stacked five or six stories or sometimes as many as ten stories high. The footprint of one of these buildings would have been around twenty-five hundred square feet, though the walls could be as thick as one and a half feet, decreasing the inside area to just over two thousand square feet. The first floor might be a shop, or divided into several smaller shops, or it could be the home of the owner of the building, in which case it might be quite comfortable, even having running water coming in through lead pipes.

The upper stories of each building were rented flats called *cenacula* (singular *cenaculum*). In some cases there may have been only a handful of flats in a building, if each floor was one flat, but it was probably the case that most floors were subdivided into smaller flats. There may have been as many as forty thousand of these apartment buildings in the city, with as many as two hundred thousand rented flats, each with an average of five or six people living in one apartment. Furniture for most people would have been very humble, and in any case there was not enough light in the apartments to enjoy anything like what we would call décor. A low shelf along the wall or a wooden bench covered with a mat would have served as the bed, and there might have been a simple table with a stool or bench. The windows would have been covered with wooden shutters, so that closing the shutters always meant that no light was coming in. Some apartments may have had balconies or window boxes with flowers and vines growing in them. The upper floors would have been more risky in case of a fire, and the top floor would have been right under the roof, which would have been prone to leaks. For these reasons the rent was probably cheaper the higher up one went. On the other hand, the top floor had access to the roof, which might have allowed tenants to raise pigeons for their eggs.

Apartment buildings were investments, not only for the owners but also for investors, who would rent out multiple flats and sublet them to tenants. However, older buildings were often unstable, and even though new building laws were instituted over time, the buildings were very close together, which meant that every building was in danger if a neighboring building collapsed or caught fire. Tenants must have lived in constant fear of these disasters, especially given that many tenants used portable stoves and constantly had to light candles, lamps, or torches to see at night, or any time the shutters were closed.

Nicer apartment buildings may have had resident slaves or slaves who made the rounds of buildings owned by the same person. We can imagine slaves bringing in water to a common cistern or sweeping out the stairwells.

The wealthiest people lived in privately owned houses called *domi* (singular *domus*), something like small villas, usually set on hilltops or in the quiet neighborhoods outside the city wall. These were large enough for an extended family along with household slaves. There could have been as many as fifty people living in a *domus*, though the slaves would not have had their own rooms. Slaves would have had mats or cots that were kept in storage during the day and pulled out into the hallways or open areas of the home for sleep at night. Other slaves slept in areas otherwise used for storage, such as under a flight of stairs.

Like apartments, houses would have had wooden shutters on the windows, but they would have also had curtains. The furniture of a *domus* would have been covered with cushions, and the walls would have been painted with colorful outdoor scenes and elaborate geometric designs. Most *domi* would have had kitchens for entertaining. A few might have had ovens for baking bread, but most people bought their bread at the market.

As a space for Christian worship, a *cenaculum* might have held ten to twenty people, while a *domus* could have held fifty people or more, especially in the case of a wealthy house equipped with a private auditorium meant for lectures and readings.

Figure 2.1. Remains of a Roman apartment building showing the stairs to upper floors, Ostia Antica

Outside the city wall, in the quiet neighborhood along the Tiburtinian Road, Urbanus and his wife, Sabina, were waking up in their separate bedrooms. A slave had rung the bell announcing that dawn was coming soon, and for Urbanus, that meant he needed to get ready to receive his clients. Sometime during the night he had been too hot and had thrown off his knee-length linen tunic and slept only in his loincloth. He pulled himself out of his large wood-and-ivory bed, found the tunic among the blankets and down pillows on the floor, and pulled it on over his head. He found his leather belt on a chair and wrapped it around his waist. Then he put on his house shoes and sat down at his desk to work on some correspondence as a slave brought in a tray with bread and water spiked with a little wine. Two slaves stood by quietly with candles until Urbanus was finished with his letters, and then they began the meticulous process of wrapping Urbanus in his toga.

Sabina was already seated in her makeup chair—an armless chair with a backrest and ivory inlays, and one of her most prized possessions. She was wearing her cotton corset and ankle-length cotton tunic. One slave was weaving a tiara into her long black hair while another applied white foundation to her face and arms. A fortuneteller read her horoscope and tried to show her a zodiac chart as the hairdresser attempted to wave her away. Sabina sighed at the knowledge that the fortuneteller never really told her anything useful, let alone true.

Sabina also had a tray of bread and water—one-fifth wine to four-fifths water. Her hairdresser plucked her gray hairs as red makeup was applied to her cheeks and lips, and black on her eyebrows and around her eyes. Sabina always insisted on brushing her own teeth, with toothpaste made of ground-up animal horn, and then applying white paint to the top teeth in the front. She looked at her wavy reflection in the copper mirror and squinted to see her teeth. She was proud to have so many of them left.

After putting on her belted dress tunic, another slave helped her choose necklaces, rings, anklets, earrings, bracelets, and a brooch for her most colorful shawl. The last thing to go on was an amulet, which Sabina hoped would give her good fortune. It was a silver pendant with the image of an eye on it. The "seeing eye" looked back at anyone who might cast the evil eye in Sabina's direction, thereby distracting the evil eye or reflecting it back toward the envious observer.

The hairdresser then packed up all of Sabina's makeup and accessories into a portable travel kit to be ready to go to the baths in the afternoon. Sabina put on her house shoes and headed out of her room, making her way to the kitchen to start the day by directing the household slaves. She could see her husband's clients beginning to line up to pay their respects and ask for favors. Although it was not yet dawn, she knew Urbanus would begin seeing them, one by one, until he had met with them all, including the widows of clients who had died.

■　■　■

Stachys was not the first to see Urbanus, since some of his clients who worked in trades came well before dawn so that they could be at work on time. But when Stachys arrived, the slave in charge invited him to the front of the line. Urbanus kept his promise and welcomed Stachys warmly, even addressing him in Greek, in spite of knowing Stachys spoke Latin fluently. Stachys called Urbanus by name and received a sincere handshake before leaving. As Stachys was about to turn to go, Urbanus said, "Join me at the baths this afternoon?"

Stachys was pleased and quite surprised to get an invitation from Urbanus. He couldn't find the right words to reply at first but didn't want to seem ungrateful, so he just nodded. Finally he said, "Yes. Absolutely. I'll be there."

"Well, meet me here first, and we'll walk there together. See you at the eighth hour."

All of this made Stachys feel very proud and increased his honor in the eyes of the other clients, who hid their jealousy as best they could until Stachys was out the door. Getting to go to the front of the line also meant that Stachys could get home in time for the last half of the morning prayer meeting of the Way-followers.

As Stachys came into the house, the group was standing with eyes and hands raised as Marcus prayed. Stachys had missed the reading of the commandments as well as the exhortation to live by them, but he was actually relieved since he found all that a bit tedious. He had a hard time understanding why the God of the Judeans and Way-followers should care whether they also worshiped other gods or how they treated other people. The gods of the Greeks and Romans didn't care about such things. It had always seemed to him like an odd kind of virtue, acting favorably to people who could never return the favor. But, he had reasoned, since this God didn't require sacrifices, he was an odd sort of God. And after all, Stachys had been on the receiving end of unjust treatment in the past, and he knew deep down that there was something better, something right, about being good to people. There was something compelling about this strange God, and anyway, Stachys reasoned, he wanted to please Maria and wanted to be part of the family that included her and her son. He couldn't quite explain it, but she was living proof that this God and his kind of virtue was a good thing.

Stachys entered the gathering just in time to recite the prayer that Iesua taught the first Way-followers. He didn't claim to understand all of it, but he liked saying it. And he liked knowing that his stepson Marcus had been there to hear Iesua teach it for the first time. Then they sang that psalm that Maria was singing the day before. The gathering was over, and people quickly dispersed to begin their day.

"*Salve*, Stachys!"

"Oh, *salve*, Scrap." Stachys was a bit startled. He hadn't seen Scrap sidle up to him, but then Scrap was always sneaking up and talking loudly when people least expected it. Stachys was often annoyed at how talkative Scrap was for an eight-year-old boy, and he couldn't get used to the idea of a slave calling him by name. "Where's young Clemens? Shouldn't you be getting back to his father's house with him?"

"My master is talking with Marcus. I'm just waiting. I guess you came in late because you were meeting with your patron, right? My master says your patron is Urbanus. Did you know that Philologus was kicked out of his guild? He can't work as a plasterer any more, and he'll never be a stonemason now. Did you know that? What's he going to do to feed his family, Stachys?"

"I don't know, Scrap. You know, I should probably go talk to Marcus too. Be well, Scrap."

"Be well, Stachys." Scrap ran over to Philologus, who seemed genuinely glad to talk to him. Philologus and Julia's children gathered around Scrap and took his hand, dragging him off to play Acorns or Blindfold Bucca.

Stachys walked over toward where Marcus was talking with Flavius Clemens, the son of the senator Clemens the Elder. Stachys always felt a bit self-conscious in the presence of the senate class, but in this case he was more interested in avoiding a conversation with the eight-year-old slave boy. However, as he approached, the fact that Marcus and Clemens spoke in whispers, combined with the wide purple stripe on Clemens's cloak, made Stachys wish he could turn around and go talk to someone else. But they saw him coming, and it was too late.

EXPOSURE

In the Roman world, life in general was precarious, but the fact that violence and death were forms of entertainment tended to reinforce the idea that some life was expendable. Both preborn and newborn life was considered disposable, and the head of a household could decide that a baby was to be discarded. Even being born on the wrong day could mean that a baby would not survive. For example, it was considered to be a bad omen to have been born on the day of Caligula's father's death, so many newborns were exposed on that day.

For most of Roman society, abortion (usually drug induced) and infanticide were perfectly acceptable. The latter was usually performed by a midwife, on the instructions of the would-be father. If the husband of the woman who had given birth had any suspicions of the parentage of the baby, or had any reservations at all about raising the child, he could simply order the child killed. This could be done by drowning in a bucket, or more often by exposure. Exposure usually meant simply putting the baby in the garbage and leaving it there to die from the elements or by wild animals. It's hard to know how many babies died this way, but we do know that a significant number of the babies left on the garbage piles were picked up and raised as slaves, often to be prostitutes. It is certain that more girls were exposed than boys, since girls were considered a financial liability.

The early church was universally against such practices, based on the conviction that all humans were created in the image of God, and therefore no one should be considered expendable. The Didache, a first-century church order manual, makes opposition to abortion and exposure one of the hallmarks of Christian identity. In other words, it was part of catechesis to instruct those preparing for baptism that Christians do not abort or expose babies. In the second century all the Christian apologists wrote against abortion and exposure.

"Stachys, you know young Clemens."

"Yes, good to see you *Dom*—" Stachys stopped himself from calling Clemens "lord."

Clemens smiled and shook Stachys's hand. "We're all equals here, Stachys. No need for formality."

Stachys could not understand why someone from the senate class would say that to someone who was not even an equestrian. No doubt the elder Clemens would feel dishonored to hear his son say such a thing.

Marcus broke the awkward silence. "Stachys, we may need your help. Clemens and I are talking about the plans for smuggling Peter into the city. Can I count on you to play a part if we need you?"

Stachys hesitated, looking down at his fidgeting hands. He did not want to get in trouble, but he didn't feel he could say no to Marcus, so he just nodded his head.

Marcus continued, "When he arrives at Ostia, our friends there will get him safely off the boat and take him to the Tavern of the Seven Sages."

Clemens looked surprised. "A tavern?"

"Don't worry, brother. It's the best place for Peter to stay out of sight."

"Are you sure? We wouldn't want anyone to think Peter is going there to . . . to be an upstairs customer."

"If anyone there knows who Peter is, then we have a bigger problem. Clemens, I need you to be the one to go there and get him. Take some trusted slaves—the toughest ones you have—and go and bring him into the city. I'll send you word when he's there, and then you'll go get him and bring him to Pudens's house. It's going to be night, so have torches ready." Clemens nodded, and Marcus turned to Stachys. "Once I get word that Peter's ship has docked, we will have to get to Clemens right away. I might need your help getting the message to him." Stachys nodded.

. . .

At the camp of the Praetorian Guard, Lucius Geta paced back and forth across the barracks' anteroom, which functioned as his office. One of the praetorians entered and saluted. "My lord Geta, I have a message from Narcissus."

Geta put out his hand to receive the small scroll sealed with wax. He looked at the seal to confirm that it had the insignia of Narcissus, freedman and secretary of the emperor Claudius, pressed into it. Then he broke the seal and quickly unrolled the scroll, skimming it for the answer he was looking for. "*Va cacá!* I was worried this might happen. It looks like he's going to give the prefecture of the grain supply to that nobody Urbanus. I can't believe Claudius is letting his freedmen give out important appointments. We should never have made that palsy-ridden cripple emperor!"

The soldier cleared his throat and looked down at his boots, shifting his weight uncomfortably.

Geta looked at the soldier. "Do you know who Urbanus is?"

"No, lord."

"Equestrian. Lives on the Tiburtinian Road, and has some farmland south of the city. Olives, mostly, I think. I want you to find out everything you can about him. And when the time is right, I want you to be ready to kill him. Understood?"

"Yes, lord."

"You're dismissed."

The soldier saluted, turned, and left.

. . .

After lunch, Stachys walked to Urbanus's house. An old slave he knew let him in, and he took a seat on a bench in the atrium to wait for Urbanus. By the time Urbanus came out, he had exchanged his toga for a cloak, and his house shoes for sandals. He greeted Stachys warmly and shook his hand. Urbanus looked around his home and smiled. "Do you miss it?"

"Living in your household?" Stachys didn't want to say the wrong thing, so he weighed his words carefully. After a pause, he decided he could be honest with Urbanus. "I mean no disrespect, but I have grown fond of the peace and quiet in my more humble home."

"Well said!" Urbanus laughed. "This house is grand, and that brings honor to my name, and my family. But it does mean more activity than I would like on some days. It's not as though we need all of these slaves. But the more slaves you have, the more wealthy you look, and that's what matters." Urbanus sighed. "I mean, how would it look if we started freeing slaves just because there wasn't enough work for them to do? But honestly, I don't know where half of them are at any given time. At the taverns, gambling, no doubt. Come, let's go." As they made their way to the door, they met Sabina, coming out of the kitchen.

Stachys bowed. "*Domina.*" He figured it was not a blasphemy to use the feminine version of "lord," since no one could confuse a matron for the Lord Iesua.

Sabina nodded to Stachys and turned to her husband. "Going out to spread your own fame far and wide, I see," she said with sarcasm.

Urbanus's smile left his face, and it was quickly replaced by a scowl as he glanced at Stachys. "You disrespect me in front of my client? And look at yourself! All that gold jewelry speaks more of you than my actions do of me. Maybe I should take it from you and melt it down, along with your mirrors, and make you a gold and copper veil to cover your mouth!" Urbanus stomped out of the house, with Stachys trying to catch up.

The two men walked mostly in silence as they made their way to the Field of Mars. "We're going to the Baths of Faustus—on me," Urbanus explained. "I usually go to the Baths of Fortunatus,

ROMAN BATHS

Virtually everyone, of all social classes, went to the baths. Most people went in the afternoon, during the "siesta" time, but even the people who worked during that time would have been expected to take some time off from work to go to the baths daily. Only the wealthiest Romans would have had bathtubs in their homes, so almost everyone bathed outside the home. Large bath complexes were subsidized by the state and were either free or had a very minimal charge. Smaller bathhouses were privately owned and would charge for entry. Some of these may have been for women only, but most were coed, and in the first century men and women bathed at the same time. Given that all five hundred thousand inhabitants of Rome were going to the baths, there must have been hundreds of bathing complexes, in every neighborhood.

Emperors and senators built huge bath complexes and opened them to the public in order to increase their own fame and create a sense of indebtedness to them. All the bathing houses would have included locker rooms, in which people put their clothes and shoes in baskets to be watched by slaves while they bathed, as well as space for massages and exercising. The larger complexes had exercise yards surrounded by colonnades that included many works of art. In the exercise yards men could wrestle, hit punching bags, practice swinging a sword against a wooden post, and play a variety of ball games with different kinds of balls. It seems that they even had a game that was something like rugby. Others watched the games, played drinking games, and bet on the contests in the exercise yard. Men and women might have run around the perimeter of the yard, and women had their favorite games as well.

Bathers went in sequence, first to a steam room, then to a hot pool, and then to a warm bathing pool. They used oil the way we use soap, and the oil was scraped off their bodies with a strigil, a curved metal scoop. After this came the cold pool, and then people dressed for an afternoon of leisure. Some of the bath complexes included libraries, lecture halls, shaded gardens for taking a walk, food vendors, and sometimes prostitutes.

Figure 2.2. Remains of a Roman bath complex showing the exercise yard, Ostia Antica

Figure 2.3. Remains of a Roman bath complex showing the mosaic floor of one of the pools, Ostia Antica

but they haven't changed the water in a while. You'll like the Baths of Faustus."

Stachys was sure he would. He almost never spent the money to go to the smaller, private baths. But since there were many of them in Rome, Stachys couldn't remember whether he had ever been to the Baths of Faustus. He walked alongside Urbanus in silence, anticipating a luxurious and relaxing afternoon.

Stachys followed Urbanus as they went from the heat and sun into the dim and shadowed halls of the Baths of Faustus. Like most bathhouses, the rooms were decorated with mosaic floors, colorfully painted walls, and Roman copies of Greek statues. There was already quite a crowd, and as they walked through the portico Urbanus waved to some friends who were playing "triangle," throwing a ball back and forth between three people. Some more muscular men were wrestling in the nude, while another group rubbed oil and sand on their bodies to get ready to wrestle the winners.

Stachys followed Urbanus into the dressing room, where they took off their cloaks, tunics, sandals, and loincloths and put them in a basket. A slave, whose job it was to watch over the clothing, stared at Urbanus and Stachys briefly to memorize their faces. Then he put the baskets with their clothes on a shelf along the wall. The two men walked out into the atrium, where the many noises of the baths echoed off the tiles. Musicians played, food vendors shouted their merchandise—Urbanus stopped for a sausage—and the sounds of people playing games, yelling to each other, came in from the portico. Men gathered around a barber, talking loudly, and the masseurs slapped the skin of their customers. Stachys tried to pretend that he was not looking at the naked bodies of the women who were bathing. Urbanus led Stachys to the massage area and over to two men standing over open tables.

"Just a massage," Urbanus said to one, as he climbed onto the table.

The other masseur looked at Stachys expectantly. When Stachys didn't say anything, the masseur said, "Just a massage for you, too, or do you want the works? It costs a little more, but you won't be sorry."

"Just a massage." He lay down on the massage table and closed his eyes, listening to the music of the panpipes and oboes.

"I hate that instrument," Urbanus said, referring to the sound of the reeds. "Too shrill." The masseur oiled them up and rubbed them down, and then scraped the oil off with iron strigils.

After their massages, Urbanus and Stachys put their tunics back on to go into the exercise yard, but Urbanus didn't feel like exercising, so he bet on the wrestlers, while watching the women play "roll the hoop." Stachys went for a run around the perimeter of the portico, and then was invited to join a group of men playing handball. After the game, Stachys wandered around the yard looking for Urbanus. He noticed a group of men sitting around the Praetorian prefect Lucius Geta, who was talking to them. Stachys couldn't hear most of what he was saying, but he did make out the words "Tiburtinian Road."

Eventually Stachys found Urbanus coming from the portico of the prostitutes. The men left their tunics in the dressing room and headed for the steam room. After taking a steam, they moved to the hot tub, then the warm bath, and finally the cold pool.

Once Stachys and Urbanus had dressed, they walked through the garden, admiring the sculptures. Stachys thought to himself how pleasant and peaceful it was. He was truly relaxed, and he thought that this was exactly the lifestyle he was looking for, the kind of life that financial advancement would buy him. He wondered whether joining the school of the Way-followers was a betrayal of his patriotic duties and expected loyalties—in other words, was it going to be bad for business?

As they walked through the portico, Stachys and Urbanus could hear speeches coming from the lecture halls. There were philosophers teaching their students, and public readings of books, and one man was reading a book written by the emperor himself on the history of the Julio-Claudian dynasty. "Did you know," Urbanus whispered, "that the emperor Claudius used to do public readings of his own books?"

"I've heard that. Why did he stop? Was it because of the speech impediment?"

"Yes. He has such a mumble that his reading is more pathetic than anything."

"I've heard that as well. And now he wants to add new letters to the alphabet? Do you know, I've heard people tell jokes about him."

"Once I heard him read from a book he was writing about dice games. I tell you, Stachys, I felt sorry for him, I really did. The man's been ridiculed his whole life, even by his own family. Why he would want to write their history I'll never know. But of course that was all before he became the emperor. Now he rarely appears in public. But who can blame him?"

As Stachys and Urbanus left the Baths of Faustus, Urbanus took the opportunity to talk to Stachys, patron to client. "I've heard some good news, Stachys."

"Oh?"

"Yes, it seems I am first in line for the prefect of the grain supply after all."

"That is good news." Both men looked down as they walked, trying not to turn their ankles on the broken potsherds and other garbage, and trying to avoid the *merda* in the street.

"Yes, but of course you know that there is no such thing as a free lunch."

"What do you mean?"

"Well, nothing is given for nothing. Narcissus is offering me the prefecture, but he expects something in return."

"What does he want, if you don't mind me asking?"

"No, I don't mind. We'll get to that. But first, you were asking me about helping you get into imports, right?"

Stachys's heart started to beat faster with the prospect of business advancement. "Yes, that's right."

"Well, I believe I can make that happen for you. But I'll need something from you in return."

"What is it? Anything you want." Stachys was feeling grateful for the afternoon at the baths.

"Good. In order for me to get the prefecture, Narcissus wants me to set up one of his newly manumitted freedmen with a position as a tutor. Now your son is just the right age, if I remember—what's his name—Tertius?"

Stachys's heart sank as he thought about handing his son over to a tutor, and having to pay for it as well. "Um, Tertius, yes."

As they made their way through the heart of the city, it was getting much noisier. People were now bumping into Stachys and Urbanus on all sides, and it was getting difficult to carry on their conversation. Someone stepped on Stachys's foot. "Great Mother!" He made the *manus cornuta*, the horned hand, and pointed it in the direction of whoever had stepped on him. "They really need to get the *merda* carts out here and take some of this away."

Urbanus pressed for a definite answer. "So, can I tell Narcissus we're agreed?"

"I don't know if I can say so right now."

Urbanus exaggerated the look of betrayal and disappointment on his face.

Stachys pretended not to notice and continued, "I have to talk with Maria."

"Talk with Maria?!" Urbanus was now indignant. "Who is the father of your household, you or Maria? Hades, she's not even his mother."

"True, but she's the only mother he has ever known, and I've seen her threaten to strangle a man who said she's not his mother. And these Way-followers . . . they really don't like the tutor-student relationship. They say the sex is taking advantage of the boys."

"What do you mean, as if it's bad for them? But how else is a boy going to start his own network of friends? This man could be your son's patron someday. And anyway, Tertius is not a man yet. He can choose to be dominant if he wants to when his beard comes in. There's no shame in starting your career as another man's favorite."

"I suppose that's true." Stachys couldn't find the words to take issue with what Urbanus was saying, but he also could not imagine how he was going to tell Maria.

"Stachys, I think that Judean woman is going to end up dishonoring you. I'm worried about you, taking up with these Way-followers. By Priapus, what kind of antisocial, unpatriotic club is this that wouldn't let a boy accept the benefits of a relationship with an older, more powerful man?"

Urbanus's own words stuck in his throat. He knew he was being unfair to the Way-followers and that their only motivation was to protect the innocence of their children. Even as he condemned their anti-Roman ways, he was strangely drawn to the strength and courage of their convictions.

"That's not all they don't allow," Stachys muttered, half to himself.

"What else?"

"Well, let's just say, if I am initiated to their table, no more prostitutes for me." Stachys didn't let on that he had already

given up visiting the prostitutes in order to enter the catechu-
menate. Truth be told, it was a condition of his union with Maria.

"What?!" Urbanus was horrified. "How dare they interfere
with a man's right to choose to . . . ! Well, it's a man's own business
what he does with his body!"

"It's true. If I join them, there is a whole list of things I can no
longer do." But Stachys's protests were halfhearted. In his mind
he knew that the lifestyle sacrifices were not his problem—he
was more worried about what becoming a baptized Way-follower would do to his ability to conduct business.

"Then you must not join them! No one can make you. No
woman is worth that!" Urbanus kept on sputtering in disbelief and
disapproval, and yet Stachys could only shrug, indicating that he
had no answer, so the two men walked on in silence. Urbanus's
first thoughts were in defense of his own righteous indignation,
but soon his words echoed in his head. *No woman is worth that.*
He thought of his wife, Sabina. *Is she worth it?* he asked himself.
Would he give up so much if she asked him to? As they walked
along without speaking, Urbanus eventually concluded that
Sabina was a very good wife. He wondered what he would do if he
had to give up other women just to keep her. Would she be worth
it? He could not easily say that he would leave her and break up
his home, even for the lifestyle he was used to. His own thoughts
surprised him. When they reached the Fontinalis Gate, Stachys
said his goodbyes, and thanked Urbanus for his generosity. Urbanus looked Stachys in the eye and said, "I do not know your
Maria well, so I should not have said that no woman is worth that.
It could be that some women are worth it." Stachys nodded to
indicate there were no hard feelings, but there was nothing left to
say at this point. Urbanus nodded back, and the two men parted.

Stachys walked toward his house, but his pace got slower and
slower as he tried in vain to think of how he was going to begin

the conversation about Tertius and a tutor with Maria. He
passed a disabled beggar and spit on the ground in front of her.

"Stachys!" It was Marcus. "Stachys, we talked about this. We
do not spit at the crippled."

"Sorry, force of habit. You know, the evil eye." He turned to
the beggar. "Sorry." Marcus gave him a look, and so Stachys
pulled out his small leather bag and dug out the smallest coin
he had. He dropped it on the ground in front of the beggar,
who snatched it up quickly. He felt bad for spitting at her, but
something bigger was nagging at him. Was the tutor-student
relationship really a bad thing? Could he say no to Urbanus?
He hadn't thought about his own childhood in the household
of Urbanus's father in a long time. But he knew one thing. He
wished he had had a father who could have said no. But if he
had had to play the part of a woman in order to become a
man, why shouldn't his son? Stachys hoped that the God of
the Way-followers would see that he had given alms to the
beggar. He hoped that this God would help him figure out
what to do.

Marcus shook his head. "Stachys, just because someone is
poor doesn't mean they're envious. And even if they are, they
can't stare at you and *make* some misfortune happen to you."

"I know, I believe that, but . . ."

"The evil eye has no power over you. You don't need superstition to protect you from it. If you're worried about it, pray like
I taught you."

"Right. Pray. I will. Thanks." Stachys went into the house, and
Marcus followed him in. "Marcus, do you mind if I talk to your
mother alone?"

"No, not at all. C'mon, Tertius, let's go fill up the water jugs."
Marcus and Tertius each took a jug, and they headed out the
door toward the nearest fountain.

When Stachys told Maria of Urbanus's offer, Maria was visibly agitated. She couldn't look Stachys in the eyes, and Stachys noticed her hands start to shake. After a long silence and a heavy sigh, she forced out the words, "You know . . ." She cleared her throat and tried again, her voice quivering. "You know what the apostles say about that. You know it's wrong."

"Now Maria," he said as calmly as he could. "Sometimes you don't understand Roman customs. This is what's expected of a boy who wants a career. Urbanus is doing him a favor."

After a long pause, Maria shook her head, with her mouth open, but nothing came out. Finally, she was able to whisper, "No." And then a little louder, "No. No you can't. You say you want to be initiated to our table, but then you do this. This is not what we do, you know that. The apostles are against it."

"But that's because they're all Judeans," Stachys protested. "They don't understand Roman customs, either. And they don't understand that this will help my career, too—it will help all of us."

"Peter will never baptize you while you have your son in that situation."

"About that . . . I've been thinking. I've been thinking maybe I'll postpone baptism for a while. My patron will soon be prefect of the grain supply, and I will have the opportunity to advance my business. This is what I've been saying, it will help all of us. But I can't take care of business and maintain my network if I'm too restricted by rules and commandments."

Maria tried to hold back tears, but soon she began to cry. Stachys let out an exasperated sigh. "Don't you see that what you're asking of me—what the Way-followers expect—it's too much! You're asking me to become a traitor to the empire. To betray my ancient traditions. Can one swim upstream in the Tiber?" Maria turned away from Stachys and stood with her back to him, sobbing.

Stachys turned and walked out of the house. He felt he could not go back for the evening meal and worship, since he was afraid Maria would have the whole gathering praying about this, and Marcus was going to want to lay hands on him and ask their God to help him with his decision—which meant Marcus would be asking their God to change his mind. Stachys didn't know where he was walking, but he walked with conviction anyway. Soon he found himself at the river, walking over the bridge into the neighborhood of Trans-Tiber. It seemed as though all of his plans were falling apart. Advancement was in his grasp, and then Urbanus's request . . . the very thing he thought would bring security now seemed like a threat. He wondered why safety seemed so elusive.

■   ■   ■

As Sabina directed the household slaves in the preparation of dinner at Urbanus's house, Urbanus covered his head and began the evening ritual. He opened the shrine cabinet near the front door and took down the bronze statue of the household god. He brought the statue to the center table in the dining room and placed a small amount of food on the statue's plate as an offering. Then he left an offering in the pantry for the gods of the storeroom as the family and guests gathered in the dining room and reclined on the couches. The reclining benches were set on three sides of the room, in a squared-off U-shape. Urbanus and Sabina reclined at the head of the room, at the top of the U. Their guests took their places, with the highest-ranking guests closest to the hosts and their unmarried daughters seated on chairs behind them. The slaves began serving the first course, beginning with Urbanus.

At Stachys's house, a very different kind of dinner was coming together. Just like they did every night, the families brought food to share. Philologus and Julia arrived with their children, apologizing that they had nothing to bring, but Maria assured them

HOUSEHOLD RELIGION

In Roman society the head of a household, or *paterfamilias*, was considered the priest of the family. He performed rituals of worship and sacrificed to several (often unnamed) deities who were believed to watch over the house and its inhabitants. The priests of Roman religion wore a hood or covered their heads to prevent them from seeing bad omens. Bad omens often came in the form of lightning, birds flying in an unfavorable direction, or other phenomena in the sky. The hood prevented the priest from looking up at the wrong time. Apparently, if the priest didn't see it, it didn't count.

Many homes had shrines or altars, and privately owned houses often had idol niches built into the wall near the door. These shrines or niches held small statues of the patron gods of the household. The *lares* were the good spirits that watched over the house, and the shrine or niche that held the bronze statue was called the *lararium*. On certain days of the month, flowers were placed at the shrine, and at family meals a small offering of food was put in the *lararium* as a sacrifice and sign of trust in these unnamed gods. The *penates* were the gods who watched over the pantry or storeroom. They were the guardians of the household's food supply. Sometimes the *penates* were depicted in the form of snakes, after the Greek version of these gods, and in fact, finding a real snake in the pantry was thought to be a good sign since snakes kept rodents away.

Some households also had shrines to Vesta, the goddess of the hearth, as well as Janus, the two-headed god, who looked toward both the past and the future. This god was thought to guard the threshold or doorway and watched over the comings and goings of the family.

For most Romans, religion was a matter of participation in good citizenship and meant keeping up the rituals for the sake of the gods' protection. What we might call personal devotion was not a part of traditional Greco-Roman religion but did come into Rome with the mystery religions from the East. In time, Christianity was seen as one of these suspicious mystery cults that advocated "personal religion"—that is, religion based on individual or small group conversion and commitment. Although many Romans were suspicious of religions based on personal devotion, they did have their own brand of personal belief, which mostly had to do with what we would call the occult—astrology, horoscopes, fortunetelling, and magic.

Figure 2.4. A typical example of the lares (singular lar), or household idols, this idol was probably used in traditional (pagan) family rituals in ancient Rome. (National Archaeological Museum, Naples)

Figure 2.5. Another example of the lares (singular lar), or household idols. Note the plate in the deity's left hand, which could have been used for the placement of a small offering of food as part of a mealtime ritual. (National Archaeological Museum, Naples)

Figure 2.6. An example of a household shrine from a wealthy house, Ostia Antica

Figure 2.7. A mosaic shrine or idol niche (National Archaeological Museum, Naples)

that this was what the *agapē* was for, and someday they would have an abundance, and others would come empty-handed to benefit from their surplus.

Stachys was conspicuously absent, but Maria acted as though she hadn't noticed, until it was time for prayer requests. She tried her best to word her concern delicately, but Tertius could sense that it had something to do with him. Marcus gave him a comforting look, and the people at the gathering prayed.

After the call-and-response "Lord, have mercy," Marcus sat down at the front of the room and spoke. "As you know, ever since our Lord Iesua ascended into the heavens, we have been anxiously waiting for him to return, as he promised. But it has now been seventeen years, and obviously he hasn't come back yet. Why he delays, we cannot say, but we find ourselves without most of our Judean brothers and sisters, who know the Scriptures and who heard Iesua teach. Even most of the people who were in Jerusalem on that Pentecost are dispersed. And now we hear that some of the Way-followers in Greece have even died without the blessing of seeing the Lord return. So, after speaking with Peter and getting his permission, I've started writing a biography of sorts—the story of Iesua, and Peter, and the other disciples. It's not finished, but I'd like to begin reading sections of it to you at our evening gatherings, so you can hear and remember the stories of what our Lord Iesua said and did."

The room buzzed with hushed excitement as everyone whispered their approval. Marcus opened a scroll and began to read. "*When Iesua left the synagogue*—mind you, I'm not trying to write down everything that happened, and it won't be in chronological order; it's really just a collection of stories about the things that happened during that time—*When Iesua left the synagogue, he went to the house of Simon*—that's Peter, by the way—*he went to the house of Simon and Andrew, with Ja—*"

Marcus's throat caught as he tried to speak the name "James," and everyone became silent as a feeling of melancholy hung over the room. Most of the group had never met the oldest son of Zebedee, but they knew that he had been executed by Herod Agrippa eight years earlier.

Marcus tried to suppress his emotion. James had always been good to him when he was an eleven-year-old boy desperate to keep up with the men as they followed Iesua around and listened to his teachings. In truth, everyone was good to young Marcus, but James was especially kind to him, perhaps because Marcus's Hebrew name, John, was the same as James's younger brother. Or maybe it was because James knew that Marcus's father, Maria's first husband, had died trying to protect John the Baptizer from execution. Marcus could remember when his father went to ask the Baptizer whether he was the one or whether they should wait for another. He could remember waiting for his father to come home that day, but he never came home. Marcus cleared his throat and continued. *"He went to the house of Simon and Andrew, with James and John. Simon's mother-in-law lay sick with a fever. They immediately told him about her. He approached, grasped her hand, and helped her up. Then the fever left her and she waited on them."*

The group murmured with elation to hear a story of Iesua healing someone. "A miracle!" they said.

But Maria was silent. Remembering the murder of James brought the doubts rushing back to her mind. How could the Lord let that happen? James, and Stephen, and Marcus's father. She worried that someday that kind of danger could come to Rome, and then what? Would she lose her son, too?

Marcus addressed the group. "Do you confess with your mouth that Iesua is *Dominus*?"

"Yes," they all said in unison.

"Do you believe in your heart that the Father raised him from the dead?"

"Yes."

"Then you will be saved."

After another prayer, Marcus said, "Tonight's Thanksgiving Bread was brought by Ampliatus and his family, from their home just north of here on Lata Street." Ampliatus handed the loaves of bread to Marcus, who held them up. "Although we meet in different homes, in different parts of the city, we are one—and we are one with all Way-followers who meet in every city, in every part of the world—and so we share the one bread to remind us of our unity." He looked at Prisca. "We remember that we are also one with those brothers and sisters who should be here in Rome with us but who are banished and scattered, like Prisca's father and mother, Aquila and Priscilla. Iesua said, *I am the bread of life. Your ancestors ate the manna in the wilderness, yet they died. This is the bread that comes down out of heaven, so that one may eat of it and not die. I am the living bread that came down out of heaven. If anyone eats this bread, he will live forever, and this bread that I give for the life of the world is my flesh. Truly, truly, I say to you, unless you eat the flesh of the Son of Man and drink his blood, you have no life in you. Whoever eats my flesh and drinks my blood has eternal life, and I will raise him up on the last day. For my flesh is true food, and my blood is true drink. Whoever eats my flesh and drinks my blood remains in me, and I in him*. This is the mystery of our faith. The *Christos* has died; the *Christos* is risen; the *Christos* will come again."

Marcus led the group in the Our Father and then said, "Brothers and sisters, John the Baptizer pointed to Iesua and said, 'Look—here is the Lamb of God, who takes away the sin of the world.' Now let's take some time to examine our spirits and

ask ourselves whether we have failed to obey the commandments of the Lord." He paused for a while, and then went on.
"With that in mind, we confess our sins to the Lord. Lamb of
God, who takes away the sins of the world, have mercy on us.
Lamb of God, who takes away the sins of the world, have mercy
on us. Lamb of God, who takes away the sins of the world, grant
us peace."

Then Marcus held the bread up for everyone to see. "Iesua
said, *Take this, all of you, and eat it: this is my body which will
be given up for you."* Marcus held up the cup of wine and said,
"*Take this, all of you, and drink from it: this is the cup of my
blood, the blood of the new and everlasting covenant. It will be
shed for you and for all so that sins may be forgiven. Do this in
memory of me.* Look—here is the Lamb of God, who takes away
the sin of the world." Marcus broke the bread and began to pass
the pieces around.

Philologus, Ampliatus, and young Clemens were ready with
their baskets. Marcus put three large pieces of the Thanksgiving Bread into the three baskets, and the deacons took off
out the door to bring the bread to the other gatherings. Then
the group settled into a more relaxed posture and shared a
meal of all the things the people had brought from their homes,
including fish, cheeses, a mixture of fried sardines and anchovies, a stew of lentils and lupin beans with zucchini, and
bread with hummus.

As the meal was winding down, Rhoda started singing, and
the others joined in. She sang each line, and the rest of the gathering echoed:

He is the image of the invisible God

The one who brings forth all of creation

For all things were created by him

All things have been created through him and for him

He is before all things

And all things are brought together in him

He is the Source

First to come forth from the dead

So that in all things he might be the ultimate one

For it seemed good for all the fullness to reside in him

And through him to reconcile all things to himself

Having made peace through him

When the singing was done, and Philologus and the other deacons had returned, they lit some torches and took the leftovers from the meal out to some people who were known to the group to be hungry.

3

THE DAY OF MERCURY

FOR STACHYS, THE DAY BEGAN in the best possible way that a Roman client could hope—with an invitation to dinner at his patron's house that evening. Stachys knew he should be happy about the invitation, but he was not naive. He knew that the invitation came with strings attached and that at some point in the evening, Urbanus was going to press him for an answer to his request. It would come at a time when it would be extremely difficult to say no.

Stachys walked home from Urbanus's house in the rain. By the time he reached the Fontinalis Gate, he was soaked and feeling sorry for himself. Still, he didn't go inside right away. He stopped and looked at his house. The house that once was his to rule as he saw fit was now taken over by this gathering of Way-followers with all their strange and foreign rules. What had Maria done to him? He could barely remember when he first realized that he would rather have her around than some younger, more Roman wife. He had moved her from her apartment across the river, along with her son, Marcus, and her freedwoman, Rhoda. What exactly had he promised her about seeking membership in the Way-followers? He couldn't really remember, and he couldn't remember whether he knew what he was getting himself into. He only knew that from that time on it was like falling down a hill, and he found himself in the school of the Way-followers, with the expectation that when Marcus thought he was ready, he would be baptized. He sighed and walked through the door as a crack of thunder shook the house.

Stachys dropped his *denarius* into the open hand of Maria, who said nothing to him. And since today was a fasting day, there would be no *sesterces* for lunch or a shave. Those coins went into a small wooden box on the shelf that had once functioned as an idol niche. Marcus looked into the box and counted the coins.

Stachys was annoyed at the group of people gathered in his house. He found Ampliatus especially annoying. Ampliatus was always so happy. Stachys squinted at him, making a fist with his thumb between his index and middle finger, and subtly pointed it at Ampliatus.

Marcus was speaking with the deacons. "I understand you're skeptical, but I saw the governor of Cyprus become a believer, so anything is possible. There's nothing the Lord can't do."

"I know something the Lord can't do!" It was Scrap, tugging at Marcus's tunic.

Marcus patted his head. "I don't know, Scrap, I think the Lord can do anything. What is it that you think the Lord can't do?"

Scrap paused as a smile spread across his face. "The Lord can't lie."

Marcus and the deacons laughed. Philologus said, "He's got you there, Marcus."

Marcus said, "Well said, Scrap! You make an excellent point!"

Stachys couldn't help but chuckle. Marcus, the man Peter left in charge of the Way-followers in Rome, stumped by a slave boy. He shook his head, turned, and walked out the door without saying goodbye to anyone. The rain had slowed to a drizzle now, so Stachys didn't mind it much. Rain made the streets muddy, but it also washed much of the *merda* into the sewer, so the fora would smell a lot better for market day.

As Stachys walked past the Forum of Caesar, he looked into the bookshops, where the booksellers' slaves were copying scrolls. He scanned the parchments nailed to the doorposts with lists of documents for sale. It seemed as though every time he passed by there were more and more books available in Latin. He nodded to Atrectus, the shopkeeper of his favorite bookshop. Atrectus nodded back to be polite but quickly turned back to his task of putting scrolls into pigeon holes. He knew Stachys was a looker, not a buyer.

Stachys pushed his way into the Old Forum, where the senators were heading into Caesar's Curia. Today was the only day this month that the Senate would be in session. Stachys could see the spear set up in the forum to advertise that there were slaves for sale. He moved on quickly, passing the "bargain" slaves who had tried to run away, with their shaved heads and their face tattoos or branded foreheads. Then he walked past the cheapest slaves, the ones who had tried to commit suicide. Such a thing had to be disclosed to a potential buyer, because it made these slaves a risky investment. But Stachys looked at them with a kind of respect—almost admiration—that they had responded to their misfortune with the noble solution of suicide. But of course, as slaves they had no legal right to kill themselves, because they were someone else's property. They must not have been the slaves of citizens, Stachys reasoned, because the slave of a citizen would become a citizen himself, if he only waited long enough. Nearby, a slave was begging his master not to sell his young son away from him. Stachys felt awkward witnessing the scene, so he moved on.

SLAVERY

Slavery in the Roman Empire was based on the rights of conquest, which meant that in any war the winners had the power to enslave the losers. There was no assumption that slaves were less intelligent than their masters. They were simply less fortunate. And there was no stigma attached to skin color that was used as a justification for slavery, so in the ancient world one could not tell who was a slave by appearance. On any given day, walking around the city of Rome, one would have seen many citizens, noncitizens, foreigners, and slaves, all interacting with one another, and would not necessarily have known who was who.

Many Roman slaves were freed, creating the status of freedmen, or former slaves. The freed slaves of Roman citizens also became citizens, so in some ways freedmen had a better life than the free poor. Freedmen often took the family names of their former masters and often continued to work for them, sometimes remaining in the household. In that case they would have continued to receive their food and lodging, but their time was not always their own, and so they (voluntarily) lived a kind of hybrid existence, somewhere between slavery and freedom. Freedmen were considered part of the extended family of their former owners and were often given the right to be buried in the family tomb, so long as they and their descendants agreed to take part in the upkeep of the tomb.

By the time of our story, Roman conquest of other lands was winding down, which means that fewer and fewer slaves were coming from the spoils of war. Most slaves in the empire were born or sold into slavery or were enslaved as the result of a criminal conviction. Many Roman households would have had no slaves at all, but some estates could have had hundreds or even thousands of slaves, especially in the case of farms or ranches. The imperial household may have had as many as twenty thousand slaves. Within these estates, foremen slaves managed the other slaves, since the owners could not possibly know them all by name.

Most male slaves were freed after about age thirty, and female slaves were freed after their childbearing years, in their mid-forties (though in both cases manumission for those outside the city, where the main occupation of slaves was farm work, may have been put off until later). For some freedom could be more of a curse than a blessing, because even though most slaves remained connected to the household after manumission, a slave who was unruly or sickly could be freed in order to be abandoned.

Slaves who tried to run away might be branded, tattooed, or forced to wear a collar with an inscription that gave the name of the owner and instructions for sending the slave back. Normally, though, slaves in Rome did not wear any distinctive clothing or markings. At one time slaves had been made to wear an earring; however, the Romans did away with the practice presumably so that slaves themselves would not be so aware of just how many of them there were. A slave revolt in Sicily in the second century BC, and the famous revolt of Spartacus in the first century BC, made the Romans wary about the possibility of slaves organizing.

Slaves were always expected to be sexually available to their masters. We might assume that Christian households were the exception to this rule. For all the prevalence and acceptance of prostitution, we should remember that any man who owned female slaves did not need to pay for sex.

In addition to working within a household or on a farm or ranch, slaves did many of the same jobs that free people did. In fact, the consolidation of land outside Rome into large slave-run estates meant that the city had an increasingly large population of freeborn workers (including former farmhands) who were unemployed or underemployed and who resented the slaves, whom they perceived were taking jobs away from them. Many slaves were not Italians, and yet if they were the slaves of citizens, they had a track toward citizenship and even upward mobility. Freedmen of citizens were citizens, and although they could not rise into the equestrian class, their sons could.

Figure 3.1. An example of a Roman slave collar (National Archaeological Museum, Naples)

Stachys strolled on toward the wine market, where he haggled over the price of an amphora of wine and then made arrangements for it to be delivered to Urbanus's house before the banquet that evening. He knew Urbanus would never serve it to his guests, but he wanted to show his appreciation for the invitation. Then he went down to Marble Street, past the grain silos, to the Aemilia Gate and the bakery market, to arrange for the week's groceries and bread for his household. Then it was time to take care of business. Stachys walked to the warehouses at the foot of the Palatine Hill and checked his store of olive oil. He casually lied to Turranius, the superintendent of the imperial storehouses, minimizing the success of his business. *No need to invite the evil eye,* he thought. Other wholesalers were bustling around, talking with the brokers, making deals on everything from paper to bricks, from cured meats to gemstones and precious metals.

Then it was time to make the long walk out to Urbanus's farm, where he would meet with the tenant farmer and discuss the price of olives and schedule the use of the olive press. Stachys

Figure 3.2. Roman warehouses at the foot of Palatine Hill

considered making a speculative offer on the next olive crop. If he could buy the olives at a reduced rate before they were ripe, he could save some money. But it was a gamble, because if the crop was bad, he would lose money.

It was just as well that today was a fasting day, Stachys reasoned, because there would be no time for lunch anyway. Good thing Maria didn't know that he was looking forward to a rich banquet at Urbanus's house on the Tiburtinian Road. Stachys's thoughts wandered back to the previous day at the baths, and he wondered why the Praetorian prefect Lucius Geta was talking about the Tiburtinian Road.

■   ■   ■

At that same time, Lucius Geta was consulting an oracle in a grotto below the temple of Jupiter. He wanted to know whether the child his wife was about to deliver was going to be a boy or whether he was going to have to disappoint his wife again by refusing to raise a daughter. As he ducked his head and entered the grotto, a priestess sat on a tripod stool in the middle of the cave, eating mushrooms from a dirty handkerchief. When it was Geta's turn, he stepped up to the priestess's assistant and offered her a special cake he had bought at a very high price. The assistant set the cake down on a small table, next to the offerings of those who had come before Geta. The priestess popped a mushroom into her mouth and closed her eyes. The assistant nodded to Geta.

"Will the child be a son?" he asked.

The assistant chanted the question to the priestess, who silently consulted with Apollo, presumably asking him to inquire of Jupiter whether Geta's wife was going to give birth to a boy. Apparently Jupiter answered, and Apollo relayed the message to the priestess, who, after a long silence, chanted the reply:

A mother's hopes will be fulfilled

This child of hers will surely live

A father's life and works repaid

A fitting reward the gods will give

Geta smiled, tipped the assistant, and walked out of the grotto. The gods knew his intention to have a girl killed, so if the child would live, it must be a boy. And the part about him getting a just reward for his life of service to the empire—the gods were granting him good fortune, which, he reasoned, was about time. As he stepped out of the grotto and into the light, he was so deep in thought that he almost bumped into his tribune, who was waiting for him. He stared at the tribune as his eyes adjusted to the light. "Have you done what I asked?"

"Yes, lord. I have men in plain tunics watching his house and following him wherever he goes."

"Good. If he is named prefect of the grain supply, I want him dead before he can take office."

"Yes, lord. Consider it done."

∎ ∎ ∎

Peter closed his eyes and took a long whiff of the sea air, letting the cool breeze blow through his tunic as he gripped the ship's rail. When he opened his eyes, the sun was bright and the sky was a clear blue. Up ahead, the island of Malta dominated the horizon. Peter thanked his friend and Lord Iesua that he would soon have a break from the sea—he would soon put his feet on solid ground for a while before continuing his journey to Rome.

∎ ∎ ∎

That afternoon Philologus pushed and jostled his way through the Field of Mars, toward the place where Julius Caesar had been assassinated almost one hundred years earlier, in the portico at the back of the Theater of Pompey. Today was the distribution of bread, and since Philologus had not worked in two days, he was hoping to get some bread to help feed his family. As he made his way to the distribution point by the temples behind Pompey's portico, he could see that many others had gotten there before him, and a few of the emperor's freedmen, along with Turranius, the superintendent of the imperial storehouses, and some representatives of the millers' guild were trying to get people to line up in an orderly fashion. Turranius stood up on the steps of a round temple of Hercules and tried to get the crowd to quiet down. "Please line up according to status!" he shouted.

A few people moved toward the front of what was supposed to be a line, but most of the people gathering could not hear Turranius. Philologus's heart sank as he saw that there were relatively

Figure 3.3. Remains of republican-era temples. Visible in the background are the arches under the street, which are the remains of the Portico of Pompey, part of the Theater of Pompey complex.

wealthy people at the front of the forming line—even a few equestrians with their purple-striped cloaks and their gold rings. The emperor's freedmen patiently showed the growing crowd where to stand, and as the mob slowly turned into a line, everyone was placed in the line according to social class, with the highest status at the front of the line. Philologus found himself standing toward the very end, all the way at Agrippa's pantheon.

Three hours later, Philologus was just close enough to the front of the line to hear Turranius announce that there was no more bread and the dole was closed. As always happened, the bread ran out before the truly needy people received any. Philologus walked away, disappointed but not broken. Still, he didn't know how he was going to tell Julia.

Maria had invited Julia to join her and Rhoda for the day's trip to the markets. Julia accepted, not because she planned to buy anything but because she welcomed the company. She admired Maria and looked up to her, and she always liked to be around Rhoda because no one ever knew what Rhoda was going to say next. She was the one who said what others were only thinking, even if it was not exactly polite. But she always told the truth and often quoted the Lord Iesua when he said, "The truth will set you free."

The women met at the Portico of the Argonauts, near the Saepta Julia, the largest shopping center in the Field of Mars. Rhoda greeted Julia with a smirk and a twinkle in her eye. "*Salve,* Julia. It's so nice of you to invite us to your shopping center. It's quite a thing to have such a monument named after you." Julia giggled, loving the joke and the attention.

"I need some new shoes," Maria said, changing the subject. "Actually, that's not true. I don't really *need* new shoes, but I want to look at new shoes . . . so I'm ready when I do need them." The other two women laughed as the three of them turned toward the cobblers. Since their men normally did most of the

WHAT ROMANS ATE

The common people ate bread, cheese, fish, polenta (either as a porridge or fried into patties), fried sardines and anchovies, beans, eggs, olives, zucchini, peas, lentils, and chickpeas. They probably could not have afforded meat very often, but when they did have it, it was usually sausages, chicken, or pork. Trade guilds and other clubs had banquets (often held in temples) that included a sacrifice, and they would have served the meat of the animal that had been sacrificed.

Wealthier people ate more meat, including beef and organ meat such as kidneys, livers, and tripe. They might have eaten boar or other game as well as goose and rabbit. They also enjoyed fruits such as pears, grapes, apples, plums, and dates. There do not seem to have been any citrus fruits there yet, though there is some evidence that people perhaps had lemons. Seafood might have included lobster, snails, and oysters, in addition to the many fish available. Desserts included cakes, muffins, nuts, and other delicacies sweetened with honey (they did not have sugar). According to some sources, the wealthiest Romans ate delicacies such as small birds or mice roasted, dipped in honey, and rolled in poppy seeds.

Romans used salt, but they did not have pepper. Their main condiment was *garum*, a salty sauce made from fermented fish guts. They put it on almost any kind of food, similar to the way Americans use ketchup.

Romans had silverware, which consisted mainly of spoons, knives, and toothpicks. They did not use forks. Wealthy people might have had gold utensils and glass goblets, while poorer people used pottery. However, it was not unusual for even modest homes to have silver, since a set of silverware was a common gift given to clients by their patrons.

Figure 3.4. Bronze Roman cooking pots, of the type used by a more affluent household or a food vendor (National Archaeological Museum, Naples)

Figure 3.5. Bronze Roman cooking pots (National Archaeological Museum, Naples)

shopping for everything except women's clothing and shoes, the women were taking the opportunity for some social time. And unlike the cobblers' shops in the Suburra, the Saepta Julia was a shopping center for luxuries, which meant that it was the place to see the newest fashions.

After checking out the latest in women's shoes, the three strolled on through the Enclosure for a leisurely walk in the shade. They browsed the art dealers, bookshops, spice merchants, perfumers, and the mirror shop. They watched the ivory carvers for a while and then looked at the silks—the newest and most exotic commodity in Rome.

It was at the silk shop that Maria recognized Sabina, Urbanus's wife. Maria approached Sabina respectfully and greeted her. "*Salve*, noble Sabina. I am Maria, wife of Stachys. Your husband is my husband's patron."

"So he is," replied Sabina warmly. "And I know my husband is looking forward to his presence at the banquet tonight."

Maria tried to hide the fact that she didn't know Stachys had been invited to a banquet—and on a fasting day. But she knew the invitation did not include her. She knew this was one of those banquets that was only for the men. "I'm sure he is very grateful for the invitation," she said. "Sabina, may I present Rhoda and Julia."

"Oh." Sabina was caught off guard. She had thought Rhoda and Julia were Maria's slaves and did not expect to be introduced to them. "*Salvete.*"

Maria saw Sabina's discomfort and recognized the issue. "My apologies. Rhoda is my freedwoman, and Julia is our friend."

Sabina seemed to relax at the explanation and smiled warmly. "May the Great Mother be good to you."

Rhoda spoke up without hesitation. "Thank you, but we don't put our faith in Cybele, or Fortuna, or whatever you call her. We only worship the one true Deity."

There was an awkward silence. "Ah, yes," Sabina nodded. "Yes, my husband has told me a bit about your religion. I must say, it does seem simpler to consolidate all of one's religion into a single god. What I don't understand is . . ." Sabina paused for a moment, choosing her words carefully. "Can one god really watch over everything? Can one god be the god of the hearth and the god of the pantry? God of the doorway, and god of the city gates? How can one god be responsible for all of that?"

Maria responded quickly before Rhoda could say something sarcastic about the impotence of the Roman gods. "We believe that the one whom Iesua called Father is all-powerful. That means there is nothing outside his sphere of influence. He needs no other gods, and in fact there is no room for any other gods."

Rhoda jumped in. "The Roman gods, if they even existed, would be limited. They have to stay out of each other's way and defer to each other's sphere of influence. What kind of god is that? That's not real deity! True divinity is all-powerful, not . . . partially powerful."

Sabina was feeling a bit overwhelmed. Maria said, "Forgive us, we didn't mean to lecture you. Rhoda here is very passionate about our religion. As we all are."

"I can see that," Sabina said. "Your passion for your god is honorable. I only fear that, should the . . . um, *other* gods hear you, they might take that passion as a form of disrespect. And that could bring misfortune on us all, if the gods should choose to punish our city."

Maria decided the smartest thing to do was to let Sabina have the last word. She made some halfhearted comment about being respectful of Sabina's time, and Sabina took her leave and headed off to the fortuneteller. After she walked away, both Maria and Julia let out a sigh of relief. Maria gave Rhoda a look that said

You have to be careful what you say, but she knew there was no point in saying it out loud.

But Rhoda wasn't looking at Maria. Rhoda was looking at a group of Vestal Virgins, wearing their distinctive bridal veils and red hoods. The one in the lead stopped their procession and looked around with an attitude of frustration. She shouted, "Claudia!"

"Here, *Domina*," came the reply from behind a column. A woman who was evidently Claudia emerged and hung her head.

Rhoda pointed at the lead vestal and whispered to Maria and Julia, "That's Vibidia. She's the elder vestal. Do you know she can pardon a man condemned to death? All she has to do is say so, and the man goes free."

"Just like that?," Julia had a hard time believing that a woman could have such power in Rome.

"Just like that," Rhoda answered. "If she pardons a man, even the emperor can't go against her—they have to let him go free."

Vibidia seemed about to raise her voice again, but her tone softened. "Claudia, where were you?"

"Looking at the silks, *Domina*."

"Looking at the silks, though you still have twenty-five years with us before you're free to wear them. And so you fell behind, causing us to have to wait for you. This is the same carelessness that you showed the night you let the sacred flame go out. I would have thought the beating you received from the emperor himself would have taught you to take more care in the future. You should consider yourself fortunate that it's bad luck to spill a vestal's blood, otherwise you might have found yourself in the arena!"

"I will never let the flame go out again, *Domina*."

"I'm certain of that." Vibidia moved close to Claudia and lifted her chin to force eye contact. "Come. Don't fall behind again." Then she turned and walked away, with her entourage in tow.

Claudia hesitated, falling to the back of the procession. As soon as the rest of the vestals were out of hearing range, Claudia turned toward Rhoda and whispered, "I want to know more about your God." And then she ran off to catch up to her sister priestesses.

All of a sudden, the women could hear yelling and screaming coming from behind them. People started running in every direction, as Julia looked at Maria and Rhoda with a look of panic on her face. Maria grabbed both Rhoda and Julia by the arm and pulled them into the shade of the Portico of Hecatostylon, shielded from the running mob by its many columns. The women could hear groups of men shouting curses and chanting something about the failed bread distribution as they began rioting in the streets, smashing and looting the shops of the Saepta. Shopkeepers were in the process of desperately trying to install the wooden panels that locked up the shops at night, but many of them had been using the panels as tables. It was a pitiful sight, shopkeepers sweeping their handmade wares off of the tables so they could use the wooden planks to close the front of the shop as looters were picking up the merchandise off of the floor. Shopkeepers' wives and daughters screamed and scrambled up the ladders into the lofts above the shops.

Maria knew that the city militia was normally only mobilized at night, so it would take a long time for them to come and calm the situation. The women couldn't afford to wait it out, especially since there was always the chance that the rioting gangs of men would graduate from looting the stores to attacking whichever women happened to be close by. Maria tightened her grip on the arms of Rhoda and Julia and pulled them to the corner of the portico. "We need to head for higher ground," she whispered. "The temple of Venus at the top of the seats in the Theater of Pompey. The mob won't go there, and if they do, we can go inside the temple. They wouldn't dare profane the place with violence. And Iesua would understand." Maria waited for a lull in the movement of the crowd, and then she pulled Rhoda and Julia out into the sun and headed for the Theater of Pompey.

The three women ran as fast as they could through Pompey's portico and past the stage of the theater. As they headed up the steps that ran along the seats, they heard a scream. Maria and Rhoda kept running, but Julia stopped and turned around. On the floor of the theater, she could see a woman struggling to get to her feet, with two men standing over her, grabbing for her jewelry. Julia shouted at Maria and Rhoda. The women turned around, but by then they could only see Julia's back as she ran down the steps toward the theater floor.

Maria screamed, "Julia!" She hesitated, not knowing what to do.

But Rhoda was decisive. "Let's go!" She turned to follow Julia, and Maria followed her. When they got to the bottom of the steps, Julia was already confronting the two men who stood over the woman on the floor. Maria recognized the woman. It was Sabina.

Julia was yelling at the men to leave Sabina alone, but her small stature was less than intimidating. They started to laugh at her, but then Rhoda ran up, and Maria, and the men were outnumbered. If looks could kill, the look on Rhoda's face would have burned them to a crisp, and so they backed off and eventually walked away. Julia helped Sabina to her feet as Sabina felt around her neck to make sure the key to the household strongbox was still there, and then they all made their way up the steps to the temple of Venus. The sound of the mob was getting louder, so they went into the temple. Sabina began to whisper to the statue of Venus at the back of the temple. She was starting to ask the goddess for help, but she was interrupted by the sound of Maria praying out loud. Sabina looked back to see Maria, Rhoda, and Julia standing in a tight circle, with hands uplifted and eyes closed.

"Lord Iesua, protect us. Lord Iesua, protect us. Lord Iesua *Christos*, protect us."

. . .

Stachys, meanwhile, had his own problems. After collecting what was owed to him for the sale of olive oil and paying what he owed, there was a respectable sum left over—a sum that he had now lost at the gambling table. He sat in the back room of the tavern, sweating and playing on credit. The table steward brought him a mug of wine—mixed strong by his request.

But he wasn't the only one losing. Another man at the table kept waving away a nervous slave who could see his own prospects draining away with his master's losses. Stachys felt more sorry for himself than ever, and the effects of the strong wine were only enhancing that feeling. He thought about the money he was losing and felt the pressure to win it back, or else he would have to explain to Maria why he came home in debt rather than with money in his hand. Then he started to tell himself that

Figure 3.6. Roman dice, carved from animal bone (National Archaeological Museum, Naples)

he should not fear Maria, that he was the head of the household, after all, and he should be able to do whatever he wanted with his money. By Priapus, he was a success!

Eventually Stachys thought of his son, and how he wanted his son to be a success. That would mean getting a good start on a career as soon as possible. This tutor could be a stepping stone to a wealthy patron. Who knows, Tertius could one day even join the equestrian class—something a freedman like Stachys could never do. Stachys thought about his own patron, Urbanus. He thought about Urbanus's father, but then dismissed the thought from his mind.

He asked Fortuna for good luck and then felt guilty about it, hearing in his mind all the things Maria and Marcus would say to him if they knew. Had the gods ever answered his prayers? Not that he could remember. Would the God of the Way-followers do any better? Maybe. Maybe not. If the gods didn't reward, then they also didn't punish, so there was no risk in abandoning them, he thought. But why just replace the traditional gods with a new one? Maybe, Stachys thought, he didn't need any at all. In any case, if he were to say no to Urbanus, he would be throwing away his own career. He would lose everything he worked for. There was no decision to make. Tertius would have a tutor. Stachys rolled the dice.

■　■　■

Across the river in Trans-Tiber, another gathering of Way-followers was preparing for their evening meal in a small apartment. Apelles, the leader of the gathering, welcomed everyone. As the people filed into the cramped space, the men talked among themselves, and the women took stock of the small amounts of food they had brought. It was mostly beans and bread, with some olives, a few pigeon eggs, and some small fish.

Trans-Tiber was one of the poorest and most densely populated areas of Rome and was the home for many of Rome's Judean population until the edict of Claudius banished them. Not all Judeans left, however, because many of them were slaves and were owned by non-Judeans. The Way-followers at Apelles's apartment included some of these remaining Judeans as well as some of the Judean believers who had once attended the gathering at Aquila and Priscilla's awning shop. It also included some dock-

workers who worked the cargo boats on the river, as well as other slaves and former prostitutes. Herodion, a freedman of the household of Aristobulus, was there with a few slaves of that house. Some of them were baptized, but others were still in the school, not yet baptized. It was a tight fit, with over twenty people in the apartment.

Apelles stepped to the front of the room and got everyone's attention. "Brothers and sisters . . . let us pray. . . ."

Figure 3.7. A typical street in modern Trastevere, the "Trans-Tiber" of ancient Rome

■ ■ ■

Stachys was proud to hear his name echo in Urbanus's dining hall as an older slave announced his arrival. This slave who was once his peer had just washed his feet and was now showing him

THE ROMAN BANQUET

In 1 Corinthians 11, when Paul criticizes the behavior of the Corinthian Christians at the *agapē* meal, he is basically accusing them of acting as though the eucharistic gathering were a Roman banquet. Wealthy households hosted banquets, which was part of the Roman culture of trading favors. Patrons invited their clients, though it was not unusual for the lower-class guests to receive inferior food and wine compared to the host's peers. Guests of a lower social class might also find themselves using inferior utensils, or the slaves of the household might be instructed to count the silverware before the guests left for the night.

The Roman dining room was called a *triclinium*, which refers to the fact that the basic setup was to have three reclining benches around a central area in a U-shaped arrangement. Of course, actual dining rooms could have more or fewer benches, depending on the wealth of the household and the kind of dinner parties the hosts expected to have. The benches had a kind of shelf or narrow table attached for each person's food. Most people ate in a reclining position, leaning on their left side with their head toward the center and eating with their right hand. Sometimes unmarried

Figure 3.8. Roman silverware. Notice there are no forks! (National Archaeological Museum, Naples)

women sat on chairs or stools, since that was considered more modest, but couples would recline together.

The area in the center might have had a portable serving table with a tablecloth, which would be moved when the time came for entertainment. The entertainment might have been hired performers, or for everyday dining it might have been slaves from within the household who could play music or dance.

Figure 3.9. Roman drinking glass (National Archaeological Museum, Naples)

Figure 3.10. Silver wine goblets with apparent olive-branch motif (National Archaeological Museum, Naples)

to his place at one of the reclining benches around the center table. It was the lowest place according to status—on the end of the bench—but Stachys was just happy to be there. He looked at the place setting with awe. A gold spoon and knife—the same workmanship as the silverware set that Urbanus had given him on his first Saturnalia as a freedman. But real gold. A carved ivory toothpick. A beautiful, translucent blue-glass wine cup. The central table was already set with a tablecloth and filled with appetizers of hot sausages, small birds roasted in egg yolk, Damascus plums, and honey balls. Two silver trays held tiny roasted mice dipped in honey, one tray with poppy seeds and one without.

"Stachys, my friend!" Urbanus greeted his client warmly and shook his hand, then turned to face the whole group. "Friends, I've spared no expense. We're having Falernian wine tonight!" Then he whispered into Stachys's ear, "Thank you for the amphora. That was most gracious of you."

Stachys knew that the wine he had bought that day was not as good as Falernian wine, but he knew he had done the right thing by giving a token gift to his host.

Urbanus raised his voice again, lifting his glass. "*Vita vinum est!*" The guests all raised their glasses and drank to the health of the host.

"*Vale,*" they all said. "Be well!"

Urbanus turned to Stachys. "Stachys, try the mice—they're delicious."

Stachys was not sure. "Do they take the bones out?"

"Oh, Stachys, you make me laugh! If they took the bones out, they wouldn't be crunchy, would they? Look, just pick it up by the tail, like this, and pop it into your mouth whole. You can bite the tail off if you don't want to eat it."

Urbanus announced that the fish in the first course were from his own fish ponds on his farmland. In addition to the fish, the first course included beef, kidneys with peas, tripe, lobster, goose, rabbit, figs, and lots of bread. Bowls of salty, fermented fish sauce were placed around for dipping or spooning onto any or all of the dishes. Stachys passed on the lobsters because they looked to him like giant bugs, but did his best to try everything else.

Stachys noticed that his hands shook a bit as he dipped a piece of bread in the fish sauce. He realized that he was somewhat nervous in the presence of Urbanus and his peers. Turranius was there, alternating between burping and lamenting the violence after the dole bread ran out. "I don't know what these plebs expect," he whined, then belched. "There are a half million people in this city, a third of whom are of too low a status to expect that they will ever receive any benefits of imperial generosity. After all, what can the riffraff do in return? It's ridiculous. Don't they realize that the dole is not about feeding people? It's about keeping the bakers baking. The bakers' guild demands it, to keep the prices up and the income flowing." He belched again. "And my own, uh . . . gratuity . . . is not insignificant of course." The men laughed as Turranius banged his chest with his fist.

"Well, we have nothing to worry about here," Urbanus reassured the group. "I've hired extra security tonight. A few of the gladiators from the training school. They're standing guard outside the door as we speak."

"Good to know, Urbanus," someone said.

Another chimed in, "Well done."

The main course came, and Stachys's blue eyes lit up to see a whole boar, surrounded by dates and delicate muffins. More bowls of fish sauce arrived, along with tiny bowls of salt. And of course, everyone's cup was kept full of that good Falernian wine. Stachys thoroughly enjoyed himself, burping appropriately to show his appreciation.

Stachys listened to the conversation as Urbanus's friends took their turns showing their respect and admiration. One of the guests asked, "Urbanus, how are your daughters? I hope they're well."

"Yes, they are, thank you for asking. They're growing like weeds—it's almost time for me to start thinking about marriage arrangements." It suddenly occurred to Urbanus that he was the only one in the room with two daughters, something that would seem odd to the nobility of Rome. "Of course we considered exposing the younger one, but I could see it would have upset Sabina, so I relented. Soft of heart I am, I admit it. And now soft of purse as well, as it turns out." The other men chuckled.

By the end of the course, Stachys started to feel a bit more comfortable among his patron's peers, and so he decided to speak up and take part in the conversation in Latin. "Urbanus," he said thoughtfully, "Does the Praetorian prefect, Lucius Geta, live near here?"

Urbanus seemed to be taken aback by the mention of his enemy's name, and he didn't know why Stachys would bring him up. "No, Stachys, why do you ask?"

"Only because I overheard him at the baths, talking with some of his men. I couldn't hear what they were saying, but I did hear him say something about the Tiburtinian Road."

Urbanus was visibly shaken. He fumbled for words, and eventually something like "I don't know why he would," fell half-heartedly out of his mouth. Then a slave entered the dining room and whispered to Urbanus. "Ah!" Urbanus seemed glad to have a distraction. "For tonight's entertainment, I have brought in a troupe of exotic dancers from Egypt." The center table was removed, and four belly dancers twirled into the room, wearing their traditional wispy costumes. Musicians followed them in and positioned themselves at the end of the room. As soon as they were in position, a drumbeat sounded and the dancers stopped, taking a pose and standing motionless. Another drumbeat and the dance began. Courtesans filed in and took their places near the guests, reclining against the men's backs as they watched the dancers.

The slaves moved around the outside of the reclining benches, serving assorted desserts that included cakes, pastries, cheeses, nuts, grapes, apples, pears, oysters, and snails, along with strong wine, warmed and sweetened with honey. Stachys didn't have much of a sweet tooth, and he didn't like the look of the oysters and snails, so he stuck with the cheeses, nuts, and fruit. He marveled at the exotic nuts, including some kinds he had never seen before. The courtesan at his back pulled herself closer and stroked his arm, which made him feel self-conscious and a little guilty.

Stachys didn't see Urbanus leave the dining room, so he was surprised when Urbanus's slave tapped him on the shoulder and told him he was wanted in Urbanus's atrium. Stachys knew the time had come when he would have to pay for his dinner. Not in money, of course. If only that were an option. He got up and went to the atrium, where Urbanus was waiting for him.

"Stachys, what do you think Geta was talking about?"

"I don't know." Stachys shook his head, surprised to be asked about his offhand comment.

"I've been thinking about it, and there is no reason he should have mentioned the road outside my door unless it had something to do with me." Urbanus paced. "Stachys, I think he means to do me harm."

Stachys didn't know what to say, so Urbanus got to the point. "I need to know whether you're going to agree to my request, because if you refuse me, I will be dishonored." The volume of Urbanus's voice started increasing. "That will put me in a weak position with Geta, and he will certainly take the opportunity to move against me. If he can convince my creditors to call in their loans, I could lose my land. And then what? I'd have to work for a living." He thought a while and sighed. "I would have to kill myself, of course, which would solve the problem for me, but it would leave my daughters to become prostitutes."

Stachys spoke quickly to try to reassure Urbanus and get him to lower his voice. "I understand. If all of that happens to you, it will be bad for me too—I would lose my patron. I have no intention of putting you through that."

Urbanus was visibly relieved. Stachys continued, "It's just that . . ."

Urbanus stiffened again. "Just that what?"

"It's just that . . . my wife."

"Stachys, I can't believe you would let her tell you what to do like this! And I can't believe that she would want you to throw away your career, not to mention the normal, expected lifestyle of a Roman man."

Stachys was confused. Part of his confusion was over why he should be so confused about this. He found himself saying, "Although . . . there *are* some in the senate class who are Wayfollowers." Urbanus raised his bushy eyebrows. Stachys continued, but his voice tapered off into a mumble. "There's Pudens, and Marcellus, young Clemens . . ."

With a sinking feeling, Stachys realized that he lacked the courage to take a stand with Urbanus, and Urbanus seemed to take his inability to give him a direct *no* as an implicit yes. Urbanus put his arm around Stachys's shoulders. "Let's go back into the dining room. Tomorrow we'll tell Narcissus the good news." With that they walked back to the desserts, the dancers, the musicians, and the courtesans.

· · ·

When Ampliatus arrived at Apelles's flat, bringing the Thanksgiving Bread from Marcus's gathering, he could barely squeeze into the apartment. He pushed his way to the front of the room and handed the basket to Apelles, who took the bread and set it on a small table. After the prayers and the sharing of the bread and wine, the cramped tenement echoed with joyful singing:

He existed in the form of God

He did not consider equality with God something to cling to

But he emptied himself

Taking the form of a servant

He came to be in the likeness of humanity

He was recognized as a man by his appearance

He humbled himself

Becoming submissive, even to the point of death

And therefore God exalted him to the highest

And gave him the name above every name

So that at the name of Iesua every knee would bend

And every tongue admit that Iesua the Christos *is* Dominus

4

THE DAY OF JUPITER

As Stachys walked toward Urbanus's house, through the Esquiline Gate, up the Esquiline Hill, through the neighborhood of the paint sellers, around the slave cemetery, past the potsherd dump, and into the quiet neighborhood, he just kept repeating to himself, *Vinus mihi in cerebrum abiit, Vinus mihi in cerebrum abiit* (the wine has gone to my head). Eventually he stumbled over Urbanus's threshold and was shown to the front of the line of clients, where he was relieved to find that Urbanus looked as bad as he felt.

"First day of the games!" Urbanus said, a little too loudly.

"Yes. Three days off from work. A welcome reprieve."

"Stachys, you look like *merda*!"

"So do you, my friend."

Urbanus's smile faded. "You forget your place—must I remind you that you are my client, and I am your patron?!" Stachys swallowed hard, his heart racing. He looked down at the floor to avoid eye contact with Urbanus. But then he heard Urbanus laughing, and when he looked up again, Urbanus said, "You must bow to me when you tell me I look like *merda*!" Urbanus laughed some more, slapping Stachys on the back, and with a gesture invited him to sit down.

Stachys was relieved but still feeling awkward, so he tried to move the conversation on to something new. "Once again, thank you for the invitation to dinner last night. I truly am grateful, and it was the best banquet I've ever been to. I only hope my comment about Geta didn't upset you."

Stachys immediately wished he hadn't brought it up.

"Not to worry, my friend." Urbanus seemed optimistic. "There is good news. I have been summoned to an audience with the emperor today." Stachys's eyes widened. "Narcissus sent a message first thing this morning requesting my presence at the palace at the third hour. I believe he means to name me as prefect of the grain supply."

"That *is* good news. Congratulations, Urbanus!"

"There is also bad news. Not bad so much as . . . *complicating.* Lucius Geta has also summoned me to meet him at the camp of the Praetorian Guard. Now, such a meeting could not possibly end well for me, but Fortuna has smiled on me today, because my appointment with the emperor gives me a reason to send a representative in my place."

"That *is* fortunate. Who will you send?"

"That would be you."

Stachys's heart sank again. "Me? But wouldn't it be better to send a slave? As a freedman, I can't legally represent you."

"Exactly. Geta cannot force you into any binding oath on my behalf. It's the perfect solution. Sending a slave might seem like an act of disrespect, but sending a successful freedman, well, in that I'm only following the example of the emperor himself."

"Yes, but you know how the senators—and equestrians— resent Claudius for making them deal with former slaves. I'm not sure that's the best solution."

"Nonsense. And anyway, this is not a negotiation. So before you really do forget your place, Stachys, accept this assignment I'm giving you and be at the Praetorian camp at the third hour today. All you have to do is explain to Geta that I cannot meet him because I will be at that same hour with the emperor Claudius."

Stachys knew it was not going to be that simple. He found himself hurrying back home to try to be present for as much of the morning prayer gathering as possible. Having determined that the old gods of Rome had never done anything for him, Stachys reasoned that Maria's God was the only one he had left. And with his meeting at the Praetorian camp looming, he figured he needed a celestial patron about now. He walked into his house out of breath and quickly joined the gathering, avoiding eye contact with Maria.

.   .   .

Urbanus's litter bearers crossed the Old Forum, struggling to keep the ride level and smooth as they negotiated the crowds on the Sacred Way. They made their way toward the Temple of Castor and Pollux, where there was an entrance to the palace with a staircase up the Sacred Slope to the top of the Palatine Hill. A gladiator parade was going through the forum, and the litter bearers had to stop and wait for what seemed like an eternity. The gladiators who were to fight the next day, along with the criminals condemned to die in the arena, were on display for the cheers and jeers of the crowd. It only increased Urbanus's stress to have to sit there in his litter and wait for the parade to go by, worrying that he might be making the emperor wait. He noticed that he was sweating as he spun his gold equestrian ring on his finger, but in the end, he made it to the palace within the appointed hour. He made a mental note to return by the bridge that connected the Palatine Hill to the Capitoline Hill, so that he could make a sacrifice at the Temple of Jupiter.

A Praetorian guard patted down all the folds of Urbanus's toga to make sure he was not carrying any weapons. When Urbanus was introduced and led into the audience room, he took in the scene, nervously spinning his ring. Claudius was seated in a large chair with a back and arms—the kind of throne one usually saw only in a statue of a seated god. Urbanus had never seen an emperor this close, and he hoped no one would think he was staring. Claudius sat askew in his throne. He had a full head of white hair, badly in need of a haircut, with bangs falling in front of his bloodshot eyes, and he looked as though he were permanently frowning due to a droop in his mouth on one side. Praetorian guards stood along the back of the room and at all the entrances. Slaves stood off to the side, ready to taste the emperor's food and wine whenever he was hungry or thirsty.

Urbanus was surprised to see the emperor's fourth wife, Agrippina, sitting next to him in a throne of her own. Since the emperor had adopted her young son, Nero, she had taken on the role of a queen—something unheard of in Rome—and people were calling her "Augusta." On the other side of the emperor stood his trusted freedman Narcissus. Both Claudius and Agrippina were being fanned by slaves with peacock-feather fans.

Urbanus's name was announced, along with his social class, and Narcissus gestured to him, indicating that he could speak to the emperor. He spoke in Latin. "Hail, son and father of gods," he began. "I am fortunate to see you so close at hand and behold your immortal radiance from my humble station."

■ ■ ■

At that same time, Stachys was across town, on the eastern edge of the city at the barracks of the Praetorian Guard, waiting and nervously running his hand through his hair and scratching his head. He had informed the tribune why he was there in

THE EMPEROR CLAUDIUS AND THE JULIO-CLAUDIAN DYNASTY

The Julio-Claudian dynasty refers to the first group of Roman emperors, who were all in one way or another related to the family of Julius Caesar. Julius Caesar was not technically an emperor, and in fact, when he tried to become a de facto emperor he was assassinated, in 44 BC. But in the aftermath of his assassination it became clear that *someone* was going to be emperor, and the result of the civil war that followed was that Julius Caesar's grand-nephew, Octavian, became the first true emperor. He won the decisive battle in 31 BC, and by 27 BC he was given imperial power and a new name: Augustus. As we read in the New Testament, Augustus was the emperor when Jesus was born. The next emperor, Tiberius, was Augustus's stepson. He was emperor from AD 14 to 37 and was the emperor during Jesus' ministry. After Tiberius came Caligula, who reigned from AD 37 to 41. He is generally regarded as having been insane, and although we don't know his mental state for sure, it seems clear that he was bullied and abused by Tiberius, and he himself ruled as a bully and abuser.

Caligula was assassinated by the Praetorian Guard in the year 41. At that time the last member of the Julio-Claudian family was Caligula's uncle, Tiberius Claudius Drusus, better known as Claudius. He was fifty years old when the Praetorians proclaimed him the new emperor.

Claudius had been kept out of sight most of his life because he was considered an embarrassment to the family. He had several physical disabilities, including a limp and a speech impediment. His health was generally poor, and many people thought him to be mentally challenged. But although he lacked social graces, he was intelligent. Because he had been made emperor by the actions of the Praetorian Guard, Claudius was more loyal to them than to the Senate. He also often gave more power and authority to his freedmen than to the senators, and he regularly executed senators and equestrians at the slightest fear of any plot against him. He felt his freedmen were more trustworthy and more efficient than senators, which may have been true in some sense, but they were also more corrupt, and the palace became a place where favors were traded. People feared Claudius for his inconsistent decisions and punishments on a whim, but they feared his freedmen as well because they believed the freedmen were really in control. This added insult to injury for the senators who resented having to submit to the authority of former slaves.

At some point before the beginning of our story, Claudius had banished all Jews from the city of Rome. According to Roman historian Suetonius, this had something to do with "disturbances" among the Jews over someone named "Chrestus." In other words, although the Romans did not yet know about Christianity as something distinct from Judaism, they heard about some conflict between

Figure 4.1. Bust of the emperor Claudius (National Archaeological Museum, Naples)

non-Christian Jews and Christian Jews over their difference of opinion about Jesus. This exile of Jews happened sometime around the year 49 or so, though we don't know the exact date. We also don't know for sure how many Jews stayed in Rome, since some were slaves, and others probably refused to leave and secretly stayed in the city. We do know, however, that the apostle Paul's associates Aquila and Priscilla left Rome at this time (Acts 18:2).

The intrigue with Claudius's wives is reflected in our story. Many people saw Claudius as a naive and gullible servant of his wives, and his fourth wife, Agrippina, especially seems to have taken advantage of him. She convinced him to adopt her son Nero, making him the next in line for the throne, even ahead of Claudius's own son Brittanicus. A few years later, Agrippina would poison Claudius, and her son Nero would became the next emperor.

Figure 4.2. Remains of the Aqua Claudia, one of the aqueducts built by the emperor Claudius

Urbanus's place, and now he could hear Geta yelling at his tribune inside the barracks. He knew that was not a good sign. Geta was not happy to hear that Urbanus had sent someone in his place, and he was even less happy to find out that Urbanus's excuse was that he was meeting with the emperor.

Geta marched out of the barracks' anteroom, stomped right up to Stachys, and looked him square in the face. Stachys fought against the temptation to avert his eyes and held his head up, waiting for whatever might come next. Geta turned around abruptly, shouted "Come!" and marched back into the anteroom. Stachys followed.

"Name?"

"Stachys. Freedman and client of Urbanus. At your service."

Geta was annoyed. "Greek. Figures. And your patron?" Although Geta had already heard Urbanus's excuse from his tribune, he was not about to let Stachys off the hook.

"My patron, Urbanus, sends his regrets. He was unable to accept your invitation to meet today because he is at this very hour in an audience with the emperor."

Geta paused to think about what to do next. He decided to get as much information out of Stachys as he could. "Is the emperor naming your patron as the prefect of the grain supply?"

"I don't know. That's the truth."

"People only say 'that's the truth' when they're lying. Why are you lying to me?"

Stachys was nervous, which he thought probably made him seem guilty. "I swear to you, in the name of my deceased first wife and the departed spirits who attend her, I am not lying. Indeed, Urbanus hopes to be named prefect, but I have no idea of the emperor's intentions. And why should I? I have never met the emperor."

Geta paced.

. . .

In the palace, the emperor fired questions at Urbanus as he dabbed the corner of his mouth with a damp handkerchief. To make matters more awkward, Claudius suffered from a form of palsy that left his speech muffled and mumbling, so Urbanus constantly had to ask him to repeat himself.

"I said . . . how do you make your living?!" Claudius yelled, as he leaned on the arms of his chair and shifted his legs. The emperor's demanding tone was an attempt to mask the fact that he couldn't remember whether Narcissus had told him anything specific about Urbanus. Claudius usually relished the luxury of leaving these kinds of things to Narcissus, and even when he was informed, the details normally went in one ear and out the other.

"Forgive me," Urbanus said, bowing his head. "I am a landowner, with tenant farmers on my land. Mostly olive groves, but also some fruit trees and fish ponds."

"Ah, good! A farmer," Claudius mumbled. "Nothing so noble as farming. Whatever comes from farming comes from the gods, no? As Cato said, the best compliment one can give a man is to call him a good farmer!"

"I also own some apartment buildings across the river, and I often speculate on commodities, primarily iron, lumber, and pottery. I have many clients, including my tenant farmers and freedmen."

Claudius frowned. "Also a trader, eh? I don't like it. Businessmen are greedy. Can't be trusted. Tell me, do you travel a lot? Away from home overnight? Leaving your wife too much leisure time?"

Urbanus's eyes darted nervously around the room as he desperately tried to think of how best to respond. He was worried that he had already said too much. As he cleared his throat, Narcissus leaned toward Claudius and said, "It is one of his freedmen who has a son that needs a tutor."

Urbanus was happy for the change of subject. His voice became enthusiastic, if a little forced. "Yes, that would be my freedman Stachys. As a slave, he rose to the position of foreman of my olive groves and manager of oil production. He was given his freedom after my father's death, and now he is a successful oil merchant. He has a son, called Tertius, I believe . . ."

Claudius grew impatient. "Where do you live?"

"Um, I live outside the Esquiline Gate, along the Tiburtinian Road."

Claudius wiped his drooling mouth and his running nose in one swift motion, obvious to all that it was a combination of habit and muscle memory that no longer required any thought. "Nice neighborhood. Quiet. Wish I lived there." Agrippina rolled her eyes, but Claudius just kept on talking. "I could curse my great-grandfather Julius for outlawing carts in the city during the day. Now they all run at night and I can't get any sleep. It's as though all of Rome is at my bedside!" Claudius's nervous tic kicked in, causing his eyes to blink rapidly and his head to twitch to the left. Then he paused for what seemed like a long time and started to nod off. Narcissus gave a signal to the slave with the peacock-feather fan, and he "accidentally" brushed the fan against Claudius's face, waking him up, something Claudius was used to. "Go to Tartarus!" he yelled at the slave, waving the fan away from his face.

■　■　■

Geta was now screaming in Stachys's face. "Well, I *do* know the emperor! I command nine cohorts of his Praetorians—that's nine thousand men at my command, all of whom share a bond of loyalty with the emperor that is born of the fact that we made him emperor in the first place. Does your patron think I will let him disrespect me like this? And what do you get out of this? What is your connection to Urbanus's hopes of being named prefect?"

Stachys didn't want to talk about his involvement, and he certainly didn't want to mention his son. But when he hesitated, Geta called for some of his men, and before Stachys knew what had happened to him, he was in chains and Geta was calling for the torturer. Stachys's mind raced. How had this happened? He was not guilty of any crime, and yet this sudden turn of events had him fearing for his life. The torturer arrived with two more soldiers, and Geta turned to Stachys, pausing for effect.

"This is your last chance to stop lying to me." Geta hissed and growled at the same time. "Soon I'm going to hand you over to these men, and then you can try lying to them, if you can."

Stachys's eyes were wide, his heart pounding. "I'm not lying. I have nothing to hide."

"Then tell me what part you have to play in this."

Stachys knew that if the soldiers took him from the barracks, all would be lost. He would probably die without ever seeing his family again. The best he could hope for was to return to them maimed and unable to work. He tried to give Geta enough information to satisfy him but without including the part about Tertius. He told Geta that he hoped Urbanus could set him up as an importer of lumber.

But Geta did not relent, and the Praetorians tightened their grip on the bonds that held Stachys. Geta paused in silence for a moment as sweat dripped into Stachys's eyes. Then, without saying anything else, Geta gestured for the soldiers to take Stachys away and turned to leave himself. Stachys's knees buckled. Then Geta stopped and turned back toward Stachys.

Geta bent down to put his face at the same level as Stachys's and pulled his head up by his hair to force Stachys to look him in the eye. "What's your connection?"

Stachys looked puzzled at first, and then a wave of realization hit him. He relented. He told Geta everything. He told him that in exchange for the appointment as prefect of the grain supply, Urbanus was going to provide one of Narcissus's men with a position as a tutor. And he told him that in exchange for Urbanus setting him up in imports, Stachys was going to hire the tutor for his son. The soldiers let go of Stachys, who dropped to his knees.

"So . . . ," Geta thought out loud as he paced, "the key to this whole arrangement . . . is your son."

In his mind Stachys was wild with guilt and fear over Geta now knowing about Tertius. Geta could solve his problem by simply having Tertius killed. Stachys racked his brain to find something to say. All he could come up with was, "But my wife is against it."

"The boy's mother?"

"Stepmother."

"And why should she be opposed to such an arrangement?"

"She belongs to the table of the Way-followers, and . . ." Stachys stopped himself, knowing that he had already said too much.

"What is a Way-follower?"

Stachys tried to think of a way to describe the group that would not make them sound political. But he was so nervous that all he could do was repeat a description he had heard in the school of the catechumen. "The Way-followers are not one kind of people, but they invite everyone to their table—rich or poor, slave or free, man or woman. They do not expose their offspring. They share their food, but not their wives."

Geta scoffed, "Or, apparently, their sons."

Stachys took a deep breath. "I am the head of my household. And if I say the boy will have a tutor, then he will have a tutor."

Geta looked Stachys in the eyes. "Are you one of these Way-followers?"

Stachys hesitated. "No," he said. "I am not."

. . .

Urbanus had hoped that the emperor would name him prefect on the spot, but he was dismissed without any decision. He sent his litter bearers away, preferring to walk home, and he slowly made his way across the bridge to the Capitoline Hill and the ancient Etruscan-style temple of Jupiter Optimus Maximus.

Figure 4.3. Stone foundation from the Temple of Jupiter Optimus Maximus on the Capitoline Hill (Capitoline Museum, Rome)

There he made some sacrifices to Jupiter, Juno, and Minerva, as well as Mercury, the god of commerce. He promised to always be committed to increasing their honor, if they would just grant his request to be the prefect of the grain supply. As he ritually ate some of the meat from the animal sacrifice, he realized that he felt hungry for lunch, but he was in no mood for the noise of the tavern. Coming down the Capitoline Hill on the north side by the Fontinalis Gate, he decided to stop at Stachys's house to see whether he was there, to ask him how the meeting with Geta went. As he came through the gate, he could see Stachys pacing in front of his house, looking down at his feet.

Urbanus called out, "Stachys!"

Stachys looked up, nodded toward Urbanus, but just kept pacing. Urbanus walked over toward him. "*Salve*, Stachys! How was the meeting at the Praetorian camp?"

Stachys shook his head and spoke quietly. "He was going to torture me."

"What?!" Urbanus was worried but wanted to smooth things over. "Come, I'll buy you lunch. I know a quiet place where we can talk."

Just then the door to Stachys's house opened, and Marcus came out, followed by Philologus. "Stachys, old man! Were you just coming in?"

THE THREE FORA

The Roman forum (the plural of *forum* is *fora*) was the public square, originally the center of town and the central place of business, commerce, and religion. Eventually, though, more and more fora grew up until there was one for every possible type of business, shopping, and cult. At the time of our story, the three most important fora were all more or less connected to one another in a growing city center. The Old Forum was the forum of republican Rome, and it included the senate house (the *curia*) as well as the law courts (the *Basilica Aemila* and *Basilica Julia*). Julius Caesar built his own forum adjacent to the Old Forum, and he rebuilt and reoriented the Senate house to send the architectural message that power was shifting from the old republic to the family of the Julio-Claudians. The Forum of Caesar included a temple dedicated to Venus, which was a bit of propaganda meant to convey the belief that Julius Caesar's family was directly descended from the goddess.

Figure 4.4. The "Old Forum"—the forum of the Roman republic

Figure 4.5. The Forum of Augustus, with remains of the Temple of Mars

Figure 4.6. Statue of Mars, the god of war. A statue such as this would have been in the Temple of Mars.

The first true emperor, Augustus, followed suit and built his forum next to the Forum of Caesar. The Forum of Augustus included a temple dedicated to Mars and was decorated with marble from all over the world. That was meant to send the message that under Augustus, the Roman Empire was the conqueror of the world.

"Actually, just going to lunch with my patron. Urbanus, you know my stepson, Marcus. Marcus, my patron, Urbanus."

Marcus shook Urbanus's hand. "*Salve.* This is our friend Philologus. He's without work right now, and he was just taking a break from the job search to come and pray with me. I was about to take him to lunch. May we join you?"

Normally, Urbanus would have been offended by the idea of a poor Judean inviting himself to lunch with an equestrian. But there was something so likable about Marcus, and Urbanus felt open to the idea of new conversation partners and taking a break from thinking about his pending appointment and his enemy, Geta. So he replied, "Of course, please join us—but you must let me pay for lunch. In exchange, I expect to choose the location. We're going to the *Caupona Solis*—the Inn of the Sun."

The men nodded, and they all walked off in the direction of the Theater of Pompey. It should have been a short walk, but they got held up by the circus parade as it came down the Capitoline Hill and turned toward the Old Forum and the Sacred Way. Eventually they made their way north into the Field of Mars, and soon they walked through the new Arch of Tiberius, to the inn, which faced the theater.

Inside the inn it was quiet and cool. A large mosaic covered one wall, with images of chariot racing and the emblem of the green team. Portraits of famous charioteers were painted into the plaster of another wall. There weren't very many people in the dining hall, and the men were able to push two small tables together, giving them plenty of room to relax. Urbanus ordered bread, cheese, cold meats, and four large cups of wine. Once they got their wine, the conversation became comfortable.

Urbanus was becoming jovial. He held up his wooden wine cup, with an image of a famous charioteer carved into it. "Who's going to the circus today? I'm a fan of the red team—though I suppose if I want the emperor's favor I should cheer for the blue, eh? If you want, you can come with me to the Lateran stables to check out the horses and talk to the trainers and groomers, so you know how to place your bets."

Marcus and Philologus looked at each other. Marcus said, "I suppose it's not a sin to go to the races." He turned to Philologus. "With work shut down for three days, it's going to be hard for you to find a job anyway. Might as well give yourself a break." There was a pause, so he continued. "We just, uh, have to go later. You know, after the executions, and the sacrifices."

Urbanus gave him a puzzled look, but he didn't look offended, so Marcus went on. "Because we're Way-followers, you see. We believe it offends our Lord if we participate in any worship of the Greek or Roman gods."

"Really? You don't take part in *any* of the sacrifices? Not even to do your patriotic duty?" Urbanus looked at Stachys.

"That's right," Marcus explained. "The games always begin with rituals to honor the gods of your tradition. But to us, that's a dishonor to our Lord, because to acknowledge the existence of your gods is to show a lack of faith in the one true God, who is all-powerful."

"Stachys, you never told me all this," Urbanus said. "But I don't know how you'll find a seat if you come in late. People have been sleeping on the bleachers since last night to get the best seats."

Marcus replied, "It's a small price to pay, to practice our devotion."

Stachys remained mostly silent. His words to Geta kept repeating in his head. *No. No . . . I am not.* But, he thought, what else could he have said? And it's not as though he was already initiated. He was only in the school, and wouldn't that mean his words were true, in a way? So why, he wondered, did he feel so guilty?

THE CIRCUS

The Roman "circus" was actually an oval horseracing track. The chariot races were the main event, although one would have seen other types of entertainment at the circus, including animal acts, acrobatics, trick riding, and many of the kinds of things we might expect to see at a modern three-ring circus—as well as some things we would not expect to see, such as public executions.

The largest and most famous circus in Rome was the Circus Maximus, which held 250,000 spectators. There the horses started from twelve stalls named after the signs of the zodiac and ran in seven tracks named after the seven "planets" (the same known heavenly bodies that the days of the week were named after). Each race was seven laps, meant to represent the orbits of the seven planets. There were twenty-four races in a day. Most of these were races of chariots pulled by two, three, or four horses, although sometimes more, and if they really wanted to show off, on rare occasions a chariot could be pulled by as many as ten horses.

Figure 4.7. The site of the Circus Maximus, with remains of a seating structure in the background

Unlike the gladiatorial arena, seating at the circus was general seating, first come, first served. That meant that families could sit together, but it also meant a lot of chaos and people coming in early, even sleeping on the wooden bleachers the night before, to save their seats. There were, of course, box seats for the imperial family and for the senators. The emperor Claudius remodeled the senators' box by having the senators' seats covered in marble.

Figure 4.8. Remains of the structure of the Circus Maximus

There were four teams of charioteers, each with its own loyal fans and its particular political affiliations. The white and green teams were allies, and the blue and red teams were allies. Each team had its own stables, supported by horse trainers, veterinarians, stable hands, equipment handlers, and even cheerleaders. The charioteers could be slaves or freedmen, and like the gladiators, some of them became very famous, and their portraits were reproduced on cups, mugs, jugs, lamps, and tavern walls. The names of charioteers, and of their horses, have been found in mosaics and on curse tablets.

In addition to the Circus Maximus, there were at least two other circuses in Rome at the time of our story: the Circus Flaminius in the Field of Mars and the Circus of Caligula (later called the Circus of Nero) on the Vatican Hill. In the center of the Circus Maximus and the Circus of Caligula, the emperors set up massive Egyptian obelisks, which symbolized Rome's triumph over Egypt and in general its power over the known world. The obelisk in the Circus Maximus was from the reign of Rameses II and is now in Piazza del Popolo on the north end of Rome. The obelisk from the Circus of Caligula is now in the center of St. Peter's Square.

Philologus took a long drink of wine. "Do you think we'll see the emperor at the circus today?"

Urbanus smiled. "I've already seen him once today."

"You have? Where?" As everyone knew, Claudius was so afraid of conspiracies against him that he rarely left the palace.

"In his throne room," Urbanus said matter-of-factly, as if he went to the palace all the time. "I had an audience with Claudius. I'm expecting an important appointment."

"Really?" Marcus seemed interested. "What kind of man is he? I've heard so many conflicting things."

"Well . . ." Urbanus thought for a while, trying to imagine what he could say about the emperor that would be generally true without letting on that he didn't really know the man personally. "He's a scholar, that's for sure. Kept mostly to himself before becoming emperor. And I hear he only likes to have sex with women, which is unusual for an emperor, I suppose." Marcus and Philologus exchanged another glance.

But Marcus seemed intrigued. "When he succeeded Caligula, it was a great relief to us Judeans. Not that we would wish for any man's death, but Caligula was planning to put a statue of himself in our temple in Jerusalem. But then Claudius appointed Herod Agrippa as king over us, and Herod immediately tried to demonstrate his power and his enthusiasm for our traditions by executing our friend James and arresting our friend Peter. When Peter escaped from the prison, he showed up at my mother's house, and that's when we came here to Rome."

Urbanus found Marcus to be an interesting conversation partner. "You know," he said, "when Caligula was assassinated, the Senate debated restoring the republic, rather than having another emperor. But it had already been three generations since the death of Caesar and the civil war. There was no going back. And besides, the Praetorians proclaimed Claudius emperor, so what could the senators do? They couldn't go against the Praetorians."

"Well," Marcus said, "someone thinks they can, since there seems to be an attempt on his life every couple of years."

Philologus joined in. "I don't understand that. If Caligula was so bad, why would anyone want to kill Claudius? The next emperor could be another Caligula, or worse."

Urbanus looked around the inn. "Men, I think we should change the subject. Speaking of politics can be dangerous." Then he looked around again, leaned in toward the center of the table, and whispered, "And never say anything negative about Caligula around the green team. Many of their fans are still loyal to him."

Urbanus leaned back and spoke normally. "Now. Philologus. Tell me, what happened to you that you can't find work?"

Philologus explained how he had been expelled from his guild and how he had gone to the distribution of bread, but the dole had run out before he got any. When he finished his story, Urbanus was silent. Urbanus had never really thought about the truly poor—the people who lived without a patron. He wondered how they could even survive, and he could almost feel the stress of not knowing where one's next meal was coming from. He felt a pang of helplessness in sympathy for Philologus and his family, and he didn't know what to say.

Marcus broke the tension with a pat on Philologus's shoulder and a smile, saying, "Don't worry, brother. The Way-followers are your guild now."

■　■　■

Back at home, Stachys was still reeling with the anxiety of vulnerability and regret from his meeting with Geta, but he covered it over with his "head of the household" routine and an authoritarian tone of voice. "Everyone, listen. Stay together in the crowds. Don't go off by yourself. Maria, Rhoda, Julia, Prisca. Shawls and veils on? Good. I know it's hot, but you don't want to give anyone any reason to mistake you for a prostitute." Prisca giggled, but Rhoda looked annoyed. Stachys thought he needed to justify himself. "Well you don't want to be groped, do you?"

The group made their way through the Fontinalis Gate and around the Capitoline Hill to the west, staying close to the inside of the wall. The streets were packed with people walking in every direction, vendors trying to get their wares to the circuses, and jugglers and acrobats doing tricks to advertise their shows later in the day. Stachys led the way as they continued along the river toward the Circus Maximus. Coming through an archway, the group was stopped by a beggar, howling and chanting a sob story about lost honor, invoking multiple gods and promising honor to any who would give him a coin.

"We only believe in the one true God," Marcus said to the man as he fished a coin out of his small leather bag. "But in his name, I'm happy to give you this." Stachys looked over Marcus's shoulder to see that he was giving the beggar a whole *sestertius*. He wondered whether that was the same *sestertius* that was supposed to buy his lunch yesterday. The beggar bowed and humbly thanked Marcus.

"We should have gone to the Circus Flaminius," Stachys muttered. "It's closer to home and less crowded."

"But the Circus Maximus will have the better races," Tertius protested. "And the emperor will be there."

As they approached the Circus Maximus, they made their way through the shops that surrounded the circus. Marcus ran ahead and confirmed that the traditional rituals were over, so they went in through the archway and scanned the crowd for some empty seats. Philologus noticed Senator Pudens sitting in the marble-tiled senators' box. He waved to Pudens, but the senator turned his head away and went back to talking with a fellow nobleman. Philologus ran to catch up with the group as they navigated their way up the wooden bleachers on the Aventine side, all the way to the top, where a few empty seats remained.

The sand on the track sparkled with quartz crystals, and the spectators squinted in the sun to see who would win. It was the last lap of race number four of a twenty-four race day. A charioteer from the white team crossed the finish line first, and two hundred and fifty thousand voices erupted into a combination of cheers, whoops, boos, and groans. The last chariot approached the final post, and the driver was whipping the horses mercilessly. They were going too fast for the turn, and the wheels of the chariot started to skid. The horses tripped, and then they hit the side of the track with a crash that splintered the chariot into a thousand pieces and left the horses maimed and the driver dead. The crowd made a noise that was some combination of groans and cheers.

After every fourth race there was a break with the Troy Game: a demonstration of horsemanship that included vaulting and trick riding. There were also animal tamers and acrobatic acts, as well as the occasional animal hunt. Today the Praetorians were hunting panthers for the entertainment of the crowd. Stachys knew Maria didn't like the animal hunts. She felt sorry for the animals, who didn't stand a chance in the circus or the arena.

"Come, ladies. Let's take a walk." Maria started walking down the bleachers, and Rhoda, Julia, and Prisca followed dutifully.

"Stay together!" Stachys shouted after them. Then he turned to Tertius. "Oh! Tertius, look! Look over there, in the emperor's box—there he is, Claudius himself!"

From a distance, Claudius almost looked regal. He stood tall, until he tried to walk, and then his unsteady legs robbed him of any poise he might have had. He limped over to his seat as the crowd got very quiet. Then he waved, and the crowd raised a halfhearted cheer.

As the women walked through the arcades beneath the bleachers, they encountered vendors selling food and wine, fortunetellers and astrologers, and prostitutes. Souvenir merchants sold cups engraved with the names and images of both the charioteers and their horses. They shouted out their merchandise. "Green team! Blue team! I have Victor! I have Tuscus!" Men placed bets on the races while stable boys and saddlers ran back and forth. The women strolled by, taking it all in but with no interest in buying anything. Then they noticed a magic and potion dealer and shook their heads. The vendor was shouting, "Curse tablets! I have curse tablets!"

Prisca turned to the other women. "Should we pray for her?"

"Yes," Maria started to say. "Wait . . ." Maria could see the back of a woman buying a curse tablet from the magic dealer. "Is that . . . ? Sabina?"

Sabina turned around and smiled to see Maria and the other women. "Oh! Maria! And . . . don't tell me . . . Julia . . . and . . . Rufina?"

Rhoda smiled. "It's Rhoda, but that was close."

Sabina couldn't help but respect Rhoda for speaking up for herself. She almost said so, but Maria jumped in. "And this is our friend Prisca. Her mother is the noble Priscilla. I believe you may know of her. She is married to the awning maker Aquila."

Sabina looked Prisca up and down. "Your mother is Priscilla? I do know her. That is, we knew each other as little girls, but I haven't seen her in years. Tell me, is she well?"

"She is, thank you for asking," Prisca replied. "She and my father are traveling in Greece."

"Because your father is a Judean, isn't he?"

"Yes, that's right."

"Well, that is no matter to me," Sabina said with a smile. "Some of my newest friends are Judeans." She looked at Maria and the others. "These brave women here may possibly have saved my life yesterday. And at the risk of their own lives."

Prisca nodded. "Yes, I heard all about your harrowing adventure during the rioting in the Field of Mars."

Sabina grasped Maria's hands and said, "I owe you all a great debt. My family owes you a great debt."

Maria asked the obvious question. "May I ask . . . were you buying a curse tablet?"

"Oh, yes. Great Mother, it's a source of endless annoyance, but my weak-willed husband Urbanus insists on continuing to visit his favorite prostitute with embarrassing regularity. She's no great thing, but she was his first, you see. His father took him to her on the day of his first shave, and he's never been able to forget her. It's not that I'm unwilling, but if he needs a break from me, he has the slaves, so I don't know why he insists on returning to that old bag of bones. But I'm finally taking matters into my own hands. The magic dealer has inscribed the curse in the lead, and now I'm off to drop it into a well so that it can sink down to Hades, where the curse will take root! But why am I boring you with my problems. I'm sure you have the same grief with your husbands, am I right?"

The women looked at each other. Rhoda spoke up. "Well, actually, Prisca and I are unmarried, but if we ever do have husbands, we plan to marry men who will—how do I say it?— Save their energy for the marriage bed."

Sabina laughed. "If only that could be true. But I think a man like that is as common in Rome as a phoenix."

Julia seemed disturbed by Sabina's pessimism. Maria smiled at Sabina and said, "What if I told you that I don't think the curse tablet is the solution to your problem?"

Sabina was intrigued. "If you have some new spell or potion, I would definitely like to know about it."

"It's not a spell or a potion. And it's not a curse. It's someone I'd like you to meet. A woman I think you will like."

"I can always use another fortuneteller."

"Well, she isn't a fortuneteller, but she is a very wise woman. Would you be willing to meet her?"

Sabina nodded. "You've already saved my life once, so I believe I can trust you. Yes, I'll meet this woman."

The next race was about to begin. This was a race of four-horse chariots. Each horse had ribbons with its team's colors woven into its mane and tail. Freedmen of the imperial house drove the chariots for the blue team, but one of the drivers for the red team was a famous charioteer named Diocles, who had won over one thousand races and had become very wealthy. Most of the people in the crowd were cheering for Diocles, but those who wanted to gain favor with the emperor were cheering for the blue team. The

THE PHOENIX

It may seem odd that a pre-Christian legend should become a popular image in the early church. But we find— both in early documents and in early Christian art—that the phoenix was an image that reminded Christians of the promise of life after death.

There are various versions of the legend, often with differences in the details, but in a nutshell the phoenix was a female songbird. She was one of a kind, so there was only the one phoenix; she didn't even

have a mate. In early Christian art she looks something like a peacock or flamingo, often depicted either with a radiant halo or corona around her head or standing in the midst of flames. The phoenix lived five hundred years, and at the end of her life, she flew back to her home (depending on the version of the legend, in Arabia or Egypt). She

Figure 4.9. Mosaic image of a phoenix (Santi Cosma e Damiano, Rome)

built a nest of frankincense and myrrh at the top of a date-palm tree, and then in the heat of the desert sun the nest burst into flames. The burning nest became the bird's cremation fire, but from the ashes the bird rose incorruptible and took to the skies to begin the cycle again.

For the early Christians the phoenix became a kind of metaphor for the resurrection of Christ and for the promise of resurrection for all who die in Christ. To be clear, though, the bird was not meant to represent Christ himself but rather the concept of resurrection. In many versions of the legend the bird that rose from the ashes was not actually the same bird that died in the fire but rather the "offspring" of that bird, which started out as a worm crawling out of the nest. So it is clear that it is not a very good analogy for Christ himself. This may be one of the reasons why the image of the phoenix did not ultimately stand the test of time in the church.

We may also ask why the early Christians didn't use the butterfly as an image of resurrection instead. The answer is probably that the butterfly was so light that for the ancients it was more of an analogy of the soul apart from the body. The early Christians did not look forward to the afterlife as a disembodied soul; rather, they looked forward to resurrection in a resurrection body (1 Cor 15). The resurrection of Christ

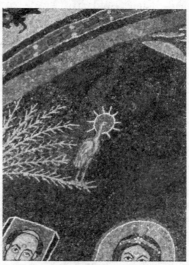

Figure 4.10. Mosaic image of a phoenix (Santa Prassede, Rome)

was a bodily resurrection, and so the image used to remind the early Christians of resurrection had to be one in which "flesh" was raised to new life. The phoenix provided that image.

We see the phoenix in the catacombs and in the apse mosaics of ancient basilicas in Rome. Ironically, the phoenix was also used as a political symbol in the city of Pompeii. To read more about the phoenix and other early Christian symbols, see Mike Aquilina's book *Signs and Mysteries: Revealing Ancient Christian Symbols* (Our Sunday Visitor, 2008).

senators were also cheering for the blue team, which made the people feel as though they were against Diocles, and tensions in the bleachers started to run high, as fans began yelling obscenities at opposing fans. Marcus and Stachys looked at each other and nodded their silent agreement. They could see that the Praetorians were already coming into the bleachers and moving among the crowd. The emperor had promised a free outdoor banquet and distribution of coins if no fights broke out all day, but that was a promise he was never going to have to keep.

"Well, I'm afraid it's time to go," Stachys said.

Tertius started whining. "What? No! The bull rodeo is up next. That's my favorite part."

"Sorry, Tertius," Marcus said. "We can't stay. Looks like the fights are breaking out early today. We don't want you to be hurt. So come on, let's go."

Figure 4.11. A temple in the Forum Boarium, or Cattle Market

They filed down the bleacher steps and out of the stands. As they walked through the arcade, they could hear the stomping of feet above them, and they could feel the vibrations in the ground under their feet. They hurried out of the stadium toward the Cattle Market. Stachys, Marcus, and Philologus all breathed a sigh of relief when they saw the women waiting at their prearranged meeting spot by the river.

"We should have gone to the Circus Flaminius," Stachys said, shaking his head.

When they arrived back at the house it was already time to start getting ready for the evening gathering, and everyone dispersed to their own afternoon tasks. Maria waited patiently until she could get Stachys alone. "We need to talk," Maria whispered. Stachys knew that tone. "What are you going to do about Tertius?"

"He will have a tutor."

"No, Stachys. I can't accept that. I know you think it will be good for

Figure 4.12. The temple dedicated to Hercules in the Forum Boarium, or Cattle Market. Most temples in Rome were not round; the only known round temples were the ones dedicated to Vesta, in the Old Forum, and to Hercules. This temple is in the area that was the Greek Quarter, so it makes sense that there would be a temple dedicated to the Greek hero-god Hercules.

your career, and his, but this is not good for anyone. It will not bring security to this house, and it will not bring you peace. Just the opposite. You Romans . . ."

Figure 4.13. The statue of Hercules from the Temple of Hercules in the Forum Boarium, or Cattle Market (Capitoline Museum, Rome)

"I'm Greek."

"Yes, I know that. But you know what I mean. You think the *Pax Romana* is such a great blessing that the Romans have bestowed on the world. You import the spoils of the colonies, and you export only your rule, and you call that peace. But you will never have peace on earth until you have peace of mind. And you can never have that in a world where young boys are seduced by older men in the name of mentoring. Rome does not grant peace—it robs everyone of peace. Even the rich are robbed of their peace because of greed and envy. Real peace doesn't come from increasing money and power. It comes from our Lord Iesua."

Stachys didn't say anything. He just turned and walked out of the house. He was confused—part of him knew she was probably right—and in any case he didn't have the energy to defend himself. He could only shake his head at the fact that he had to walk out of his own house to clear his head and think.

■　■　■

After the opening prayers and the petitions for the Lord's mercy, Marcus took out a scroll. As he opened it, the door swung in slowly. It was clear that whoever was opening the door was trying to do it quietly to avoid notice, but that only made it squeak all the more. Everyone turned to see who it was. An old woman slowly entered the room. She was bent over, walking with a cane, and she seemed to move only with great difficulty, but she smiled a great toothless smile, and her eyes held the light of a woman in her prime. Everyone in the room became excited and buzzed with whispers. "Susannah! It's Susannah!"

She was followed by another woman. It was Sabina, feeling very sheepish and out of place. Marcus smiled and began to read:

Iesua said to his disciples, "How hard it is for the rich to enter the kingdom of God." The disciples were amazed at his words, so he said it again, "Children, how hard it is to enter the kingdom of God. It is easier for a camel to pass through the eye of a needle than for a rich man to enter the kingdom of God." They were even more astonished at this and asked, "Then who can be saved?" Iesua looked at them and said, "For people it is impossible, but not for God. All things are possible for God."

Marcus closed the scroll. "All things are possible for God . . . except to lie, right, Scrap?" Scrap smiled and nodded. "Brothers and sisters," Marcus continued, "here in Rome, we can't sell all of our possessions and share all things in common, mostly because some of us are slaves and are owned by other people—some of you don't even own yourselves, let alone possessions. And yet the poor among us are only one apartment fire away from homelessness and starvation. And every day, there are more and more of the hungry and homeless in Rome. Farmers who have lost their land to debt and to the farm consolidation of the corporations. Widows who were left with no inheritance because they could not have a registered marriage. Orphan infants rescued from the garbage piles. The laws protect the rich and powerful but restrict the poor.

"Freedom is a luxury that the rich think they have earned, by which they mean they have inherited it. But they don't know about real freedom. That's the freedom we have in Iesua, the freedom that comes from forgiveness. Friends, we know that the Romans do not believe that all people are created in the image of God. They believe that some were created to rule, and the rest were created to be ruled and to be expendable, for the profit and entertainment of the nobility. They do not believe that all people are created equal, but we do believe that. Whether a person is rich or poor, free, freed, or slave, or man or woman—Iesua loves us all."

Sabina was amazed at Marcus's words. They were so plain that they shouldn't have had any appeal to her, and yet her mind was more focused on these words than it had ever been on any words before. Why did such a subversive, antisocial speech make her heart sink in her chest? Didn't these people believe in the stability of the social order that was found in accepting one's station in life? Why did she find such a message attractive?

Young Clemens spoke up. "Is it a sin to be wealthy?"

"No," Marcus reassured him. "But it is a sin to hide your wealth, to refuse to share it, and to treat the wealthy better than you treat the poor. Here at the table of the Lord, rich and poor are brothers and sisters."

The tables were set with the different food that the people had brought. Maria announced, "Everyone . . . we're very grateful for Ampliatus and his family for providing the chickens tonight. They've brought enough for everyone to have some, so don't be shy."

■   ■   ■

When Philologus arrived with the Thanksgiving Bread at the house of Pudens, the senator met him at the door. "Philologus, I have to ask you to forgive me."

"What for?" Philologus knew what for.

"Today at the circus, you waved at me, but I ignored you. I purposely looked away because if I had waved back, my colleagues in the Senate would have asked how I knew you. And there's no reason I should, except that we are brothers at the Lord's table. I'm sorry, my brother, I acted out of fear."

Philologus smiled. He was just happy to know that it wasn't because Pudens disliked him. "Of course. Forgiven, and forgotten."

■   ■   ■

Stachys snuck in at the end of the meal. He tried to come in unnoticed, but Ampliatus drew attention to him, with a smile as wide as his face. "*Salve*, Stachys. It's good to see you. Help yourself to some chicken. There's enough for everyone."

Stachys suppressed his annoyance as best he could, but his mind was distracted, and he couldn't help the sarcasm coming out in his voice. "Well, thank the Lord!"

Stachys found he couldn't eat. Ampliatus's chicken disgusted him. The bread offended him. The fish sickened him. He could only nurse the confusion in his head that came from being caught in the middle of Urbanus's demands, Geta's threats, and Maria's pleading. If he said yes to Urbanus, he would advance his career, but the increased visibility would put him in danger with Geta and who knows how many unknown envious competitors. Not to mention the fact that he wouldn't be welcome in Maria's bed again for a very long time, if ever. But if he said no to Urbanus, he would likely lose his patron as well as his livelihood. He could please his wife but lose his home. How could he get through this and preserve his honor?

Stachys worried that it was possible his situation could get to the point where suicide would be the only dignified solution left to him. He had hoped to live at least to the age of fifty, but perhaps that was an unrealistic expectation. A life of disgrace was worse than death, after all. He resolved to leave his own death as a last resort, an option open to him that, if worse came to worst, would preserve his honor in the eyes of his fellow citizens. But what about in the eyes of Maria and her God? He shook off that thought as he heard the gathering sing:

There is one God, the Father

From whom all things come

And we will return to him

There is one Lord, Iesua the Christos

Through whom all things come

And we will return through him

5

THE DAY OF VENUS

PHILOLOGUS LOOKED DOWN into his clay cup. It held only water, without even the slightest bit of wine to give it flavor. He could remember his last thought before falling asleep the night before. He and his family had successfully dodged death for one more day. And now a new day was beginning. But how long could anyone postpone starvation and death? How long could a man go on living in fear of everything from crazy emperors to crumbling buildings? Philologus had been a plasterer, and he knew how many cracks in the buildings should have been repaired but were only plastered over. He knew how dangerous it was just to walk down the narrow streets or stand between two buildings.

"I hate plain water." The frustration of unemployment was coming out in complaints about the smallest things.

Julia looked at him disapprovingly. She kept looking at him, seated there on the bench at their small wooden table, but she spoke to her children. "Children, what your father is doing right now is called complaining. Rather than being thankful that he has water, he is grumbling because he has no wine."

Philologus sighed. "It seems like we just had a fasting day two days ago."

"We did, beloved. But today is a fasting day, too. Which is convenient for us, since we have no money for lunch anyway. So you see, the Lord has blessed us."

Philologus looked at Julia. She was smirking. She was not that naive, after all, but her comment did sting, since he took it as his responsibility to provide for his family. Although it was day two of the games today, there would be no circus for Philologus. He had to find work.

■ ■ ■

Stachys was shown to the front of the line of clients in Urbanus's atrium, and Urbanus got right down to business. "I have another audience with the emperor today."

"Do you think he will name you as prefect?"

"I believe he will. But if he does, Geta will be more envious than ever. And if he does not, I'll be dishonored, and Geta is still a threat. But I have a plan. I need you to meet me tonight, at the sixteenth hour. The warehouses at the foot of the Aventine, by the river. Don't be late."

■ ■ ■

At that same moment Lucius Geta paced in his anteroom. A Praetorian rushed in and startled him.

"My lord Geta."

"Yes, what is it?"

"It's your wife. She has begun the first pains of delivery. May Mars give you a son!"

"Ah. A son, indeed. By Priapus, I had to expose three girls to get my boy—another would be good. Take a message to her." The soldier reached into a leather messenger bag and pulled out a wax tablet set in a double wooden frame. He took out a stylus and stood at attention, waiting to take dictation. Geta thought about what to say. "To my wife. I hear you are about to deliver the child. May Janus protect you. I regret that business prevents me from being present at the child's birth. If it is a boy, keep it. Your husband."

The soldier closed the frame and put the tablet and stylus into his bag. Geta frowned. "She's not going to like my decision. But there you have it. Now take it to her." The soldier saluted and turned to leave.

"Wait." The soldier turned back toward Geta. "Don't write this down, but give a message to the midwife, so that my wife doesn't hear it."

"Yes, lord."

"If it's a girl, it's to be drowned. Not exposed. I don't want it picked up by a pimp and raised in a brothel. Now go."

"Yes, lord." And with that, the soldier was gone, and Geta resumed his pacing.

■   ■   ■

When Stachys told Maria he would be going out after the evening meeting, she seemed visibly shaken. "You're going out at night? After we lock the doors?"

NIGHT IN ROME

It's hard for those of us who live in populated areas to imagine just how dark it would have been at night in the ancient world. Without street-lights, or even the ambient light of a city's skyline, there was only the moon. On top of that, there was very little of what we would call police presence at night in the city of Rome. Although there were squads of night watchmen who walked the streets, a person had to be caught in the act of committing a crime in order to be prosecuted—which made criminals quite bold at night. In fact, even the murder of a noncitizen would never have been investigated. So nighttime was considered the realm of robbers, muggers, and killers, who knew that there was no system in place to investigate crimes after the fact.

On the other hand, nighttime was when all the transportation of goods took place in Rome. By law, no cart traffic was allowed within the city wall during the day, with the exception of some construction carts and anything under the authority of the Vestal Virgins. So everything had to be moved at night. Porters, cart drivers, and construction workers shouted and swore as carts pounded and scraped the paving stones of the major roads, and the fire brigades ran to and from the nightly apartment fires around the city.

Figure 5.1. A Roman street with shops at night, Markets of Trajan, Rome

Therefore, although it was very dark at night, it was also very noisy. Nevertheless, going out at night was considered a dangerous enterprise. Most people stayed inside behind locked doors after dark, and those who were out at a banquet or other social gathering until after dark would normally plan to have slaves waiting for them with torches to light the way and to serve as bodyguards.

"I don't have a choice. My patron requested me. What can I do?"

"Well, we know you can't say no to him," she said with contempt.

"That's not fair."

"You're going to talk to me about fair?" Maria paused, then sighed. "Listen, it's dangerous out there at night. And there's no moon tonight, so it's going to be completely dark. You'll need to take a torch. You're not going alone, are you?"

"I have to."

Marcus said goodbye to the people who were leaving the morning prayer gathering. Then he turned to those who had stayed. "All right, now. Time for school. Let's sit over here. Stachys, come on, we're having school."

Stachys sighed. Although he had decided to postpone his baptism, he couldn't come up with an excuse to get out of the school meeting, and he certainly didn't want to get into a discussion about his decision with Marcus. So he walked over to the group without saying anything, determined to sit in the back and stay quiet.

Marcus faced the catechumens. "We've been talking about the expectations of a baptized Way-follower, because, well, you have to know what you're committing to. You know that the lifestyle of a Way-follower is very different from what most people are used to—and what most people would expect of a patriotic Roman. I think that's why we're called Way-followers—we follow a different way and live a different lifestyle. There are so many things that the Romans do, and even consider good, that we are not allowed to do. And we've already talked about a lot of them. But today I want to tell you that they all come from one place, or they all stem from one source: idolatry. The worship of false gods is the root of all of the sins of the Romans. And believe me, I understand, the Roman gods can be very attractive. Say the right words, and they promise you will have control over your friends

ROMAN VIRTUES

The classic Roman virtues, which come from Stoic philosophy, were wisdom, courage, self-control, and justice. These may sound like they could be compatible with Christian morals, but the Roman virtues were conceived only with the upper classes in mind and were understood in such a way that they served the needs of the powerful. In other words, Roman virtues had no thought about helping those less fortunate; they were really intended to equip those with authority to make rational decisions that would benefit them in the long run. So while a Christian is expected to practice self-control, the motivation is so that we do not sin against God and others and so that we don't take advantage of others. The Roman virtue of self-control was motivated by a utilitarian self-interest: I should discipline myself now so that I will benefit later (not so that others will benefit from my discipline).

Another difference between Roman virtues and Christian morals is seen in the difference between Roman philanthropy and Christian charity. Roman philanthropy consisted of the tradition of making donations to the city of Rome, often in the form of building monuments or sponsoring games and shows—but all in the interest of increasing the fame and honor of the donor. Christian charity, on the other hand, was based on the conviction that all people are created in the image of God and are therefore created equal—a belief that the Romans would have thought ridiculous. To read more about the contrast and conflict between early Christian morality and the ethics of the Romans, see my book *How Christianity Saved Civilization: And Must Do So Again,* cowritten with Mike Aquilina (Sophia Institute Press, 2019).

and enemies, and lovers will flock to you. The problem with that is, they can't keep their promises because they're just made of painted wood, or stone. They don't exist. But if you believe that they do, well, if you believe that one lie, you'll believe them all. You'll believe that sex and gossip and humiliation and death are all forms of entertainment. If you worship creation rather than the Creator, it's a short step to worshiping yourself."

As Stachys sat in the school meeting listening to Marcus criticize every Roman value he had ever been taught, Urbanus went again to the Palatine Hill to meet with the emperor. This time Claudius was not in the throne room. He was in a smaller audience room, reclining on a brass couch with a down mattress and pillows. Urbanus noted that he was being invited farther into the residential area of the palace than last time, and that must be a good omen. He looked with admiration at the elaborately painted walls, with faux architectural elements, garlands, wreaths, and great scenes of banquets and picnics from floor to ceiling.

Figure 5.2. Painted wall from a Roman villa (National Roman Museum at Palazzo Massimo, Rome)

Figure 5.3. Painted walls from a Roman villa (National Roman Museum at Palazzo Massimo, Rome)

"Hail, son and father of gods . . ."

"Yes, yes," Claudius interrupted. He paused, then grimaced, holding his stomach. Then he leaned to one side and broke wind loudly. The food tasters rolled their eyes, and a few of the attendants tried their best to stifle their giggles. Agrippina was visibly embarrassed, and Narcissus looked impatient. Claudius seemed annoyed at the various reactions. He shouted at Narcissus, even though Narcissus was close by.

"Narcissus!"

"Yes, lord?"

"Take dictation!"

Narcissus called for a wax tablet and stylus. "Ready, lord."

"To my co-consul, Antistius Vetus, and the senate. Brother senators, since it is unhealthy and most grievous to the internal organs to suppress the wind which comes from the natural processes of digestion, I propose and advise the Senate to affirm that it is a natural, and most acceptable thing, for a

Roman man to fart at will, an act which should in no way draw attention to itself, nor result in ridicule, derision, or revulsion. Signed and sealed, et cetera et cetera, Tiberius Claudius Caesar Augustus Germanicus."

The emperor turned back to Urbanus. "Narcissus advises me to make you prefect of the grain supply." There was a long pause. Urbanus didn't know whether to express gratitude or desire for the position, but it didn't matter because he couldn't put any words together in time for a response. "Well? Do you want the position?"

"Yes, lord. I would be honored to hold that post."

"Of course *you* would be honored. That's obvious. But would *I* be honored by you holding the post? That's what I'm trying to figure out. And I want to do it quickly so I can make my sacrifice to Mars and still get to the arena for today's executions. By Priapus, it seems like the games get more and more boring with every passing year. So . . . what will you do if you are prefect of the grain supply?"

Urbanus thought for a moment. He wasn't prepared for the emperor's question. A thought popped into his head, but he immediately dismissed it. He struggled to think of something else to say, but the silence was becoming uncomfortable, and the emperor was becoming visibly annoyed. Then he said it. It surprised him to hear the thought that he had just dismissed coming out of his mouth. But it just came out, and there it was. There was no taking it back. "I met a man named Philologus who can't feed his family, and when he went for the distribution of bread, they ran out before he got any. I would want to make sure a man like Philologus can feed his family."

.   .   .

Back at Stachys's house, the school meeting ended with a prayer, and the catechumens dispersed. Stachys noticed that Maria was packing a picnic lunch. "What's this?" he asked her.

Maria gave him a look. "Don't you know what today is?"

"Should I?"

"Tertius's mother? The anniversary of her death? We're going to the cemetery. And you're coming too."

Stachys sighed. Normally he was grateful that Maria remembered dates. But he was feeling overwhelmed and more than a little distant from his wife. He nodded his agreement.

They walked in silence, with Tertius leading the way, across the Field of Mars. A cohort of new legionary recruits was practicing marching drills on the field to the west of the Theater of Pompey, so they had to walk around the soldiers to the south, then go north along the river to cross over to the Vatican Hill. Tertius was momentarily distracted by a group of mimes doing a skit in the street to advertise their show later that day. Then

Figure 5.4. Remains of a Roman mausoleum with urn niches, Ostia Antica

a funeral procession blocked their path, and they had to wait while the oboe players and professional mourners walked slowly by, the mourners in their mourning robes with their purposely messed-up hair. Eventually they made their way up the hill, to the cemetery at the back of the Circus of Caligula, and came to Urbanus's family tomb. As a freedman of the household of Urbanus, Stachys and his family were entitled to be buried in the mausoleum.

Figure 5.5. Fragment of a wall painting from a mausoleum with urn niches. Notice the spaces for the names of the deceased below where the niches would have been. The names themselves have faded. (National Roman Museum at Palazzo Massimo, Rome)

Stachys lit a lamp, and the three of them ducked their heads and went into the cubicle that held the burial place of his first wife. Stachys had spent a small fortune for the sarcophagus, carved with elaborate scenes of Elysium, with its gardens and grapevines. There were two faces carved into the side: the face of Tertius's mother and a blank face, waiting for the sculptor to carve the features of Stachys's own face when he died. Stachys's heart turned a bit melancholy when he saw it. The death of his first wife had been hard on him, especially with Tertius losing his mother at barely one year old. Stachys thought about the prospect of his own death, and although suicide would preserve his honor, he knew it would break his family's hearts, and so he knew he could never go through with it. But he remained stoic and showed no emotion.

Maria opened the basket of food and set out lunch on the lid of the sarcophagus.

"Can I do it?" Tertius asked.

Stachys nodded. "Of course. Go ahead."

Maria poured some wine into a small clay cup. Tertius took the cup and poured the wine down the libation hole in the sarcophagus lid. The three of them ate their lunch without much conversation, except when Tertius begged Stachys to tell stories about his mother. It was always awkward for Stachys to tell stories about his first wife that would please his son without making his new wife uncomfortable. But he

Figure 5.6. Libation hole in the lid of a grave marker. On the anniversary of a loved one's death, people gathered at the burial site for a picnic called a refrigerium, and part of the ritual included pouring some wine into the hole for the deceased. (Capitoline Museum, Rome)

had come to appreciate Maria for taking part in the memorial meals. He looked at his son, who seemed so young. Still such a little boy. So young to be given to a tutor. Stachys could feel that his heart was softening, but he steeled his resolve against changing his mind.

■   ■   ■

At Urbanus's home on the hill, Sabina was getting ready for an afternoon at the theater. She relished the process of choosing the brightest colors to wear and the most expensive jewelry. Urbanus was always telling her to tone it down, for fear of the evil eye, but she never listened—in fact, his pleas only made her exercise the freedom of her noble will all the more. She smiled at her ability to disregard her husband's wishes as her slave put on her gold bracelets. She was of the senate class, after all, and he was only an equestrian. Sabina wondered to herself whether she would have married Urbanus if she had had more time to choose a second husband. Had she settled for him just because the end of the mourning period was coming up, with its two-year remarriage deadline? But the more she thought about it, the better he looked to her in comparison to other men. He was a good man, after all, and a good husband. He provided for her well, but more important, he took good care of her. No, she decided as she rested her sun parasol on her shoulder, she had not settled for him. She had chosen him.

Sabina had invited Maria, Rhoda, Julia, and Prisca to join her at the baths, but they had declined. She thought it was odd that these Way-follower women, who were mostly poor, would spend the money to go to the private women-only baths. Where was the fun in that? But at least she could look forward to their company at the theater. Sabina had used the fact that they declined her invitation to the baths to coerce them into accepting an invitation to the theater. The women had been very reluctant at first but eventually relented and agreed to attend. Sabina smiled to her herself with pride over her small victory. Today promised to be much more entertaining than spending time with the stuffy old senators' wives.

. . .

Philologus noticed that Julia was preparing to go out and worried that she might be planning to spend the last of their money. She assured him that it wasn't going to cost them anything, but he pressed for details. When she finally admitted where she was going, he shook his head. "You're going to the *theater*? I really wish you wouldn't. You know Marcus says that Way-followers shouldn't go to the theater. They have the Bacchus dedication, with the live sex show, and then the plays are all about laughing at other people's misfortunes. That's not what we do, Julia."

"We're going to arrive after the dedication. And the rest is not that bad. Anyway, the noble lady Sabina invited us, and we're trying to tell her about Iesua."

"But how can you tell her about Iesua when you're at the theater? Isn't that kind of a mixed message? I heard they have a play called *Cinyras and Myrrha* about father-daughter incest!"

"I don't know about that play. I think we're going to see *Verae Matronae Romae*. I want to find out what kind of schemes Agrippina is up to."

"It's not real, Julia, you know that. Whatever they do on stage, it's not what the real Agrippina is doing. It's a farce. Do you think the emperor's wife is really involved in all that intrigue, committing adultery, and murder?"

"Just take care of the children until I get back, my dove. " And with that Julia was out the door.

THE THEATER

The Roman theater was a decaying remnant of the Greek theater. Whereas Greek theater had two kinds of plays—tragedy and comedy— Roman theater replaced the comedy with an erotic musical farce known as the pantomime. Tragic plays continued to use masks and followed the tradition of all roles being played by male actors, but the pantomime did away with the masks and included actresses, who were expected to provide a lot of nudity.

Pantomimes often entertained audiences by humiliating real people and famous families. They included elements of slapstick and vaudeville-like song and dance as well as real sex and fighting on stage. By the late first century there were also snuff plays, in which a condemned criminal could be cast in a role that would end in the character's—and the criminal's—death on stage.

Greek theaters were usually built into hills, so that the audience sat on the rise of the hill, giving everyone a good view of the stage. However, the Romans, being more advanced architects and builders, did not need to build on a hill but rather built up the theater as a freestanding structure or as part of a larger complex. Like gladiatorial arenas, theaters had separate seating sections for men and women.

Theater season was April to November, taking a break in the colder months since the theaters were open to the sky. Like the games and other shows, plays always began with pagan ritual, and so they not only paid homage to the Greco-Roman gods but also became a kind of participation in idolatrous worship.

The theater was one of the few places where the common people had a voice. In the safety of numbers, a theater audience could shout slogans expressing political dissatisfaction and even boo the emperor. However, that could backfire if the crowd became riotous; the emperor Caligula once massacred an entire theater audience because they protested a tax increase.

Early Christian writings tried (often in vain) to get Christians to stop going to the plays and other spectacles, since the humiliation, fighting, and public executions only served to add to the cheapening of human life and dignity. As several early Christian theologians wrote, if Christians are not allowed to do something, then they are also not allowed to watch it.

At the time of our story, there were at least three theaters in Rome. The Theater of Balbus was near the Circus Flaminius on the south side of the Field of Mars. The Theater of Pompey was part of a large complex in the center of the Field of Mars. The Theater of Marcellus was near where the city wall met the River Tiber. This latter theater was later the model for the Colosseum.

Figure 5.7. Remains of a Roman theater, Ostia Antica

The women all met at the entrance to the Theater of Balbus, next to the Circus Flaminius. They went in and sat in the women's section, as close to the stage as they could and still have enough room to sit together. The play was beginning, and Sabina spoke to the group in a whisper. She was playing the hostess, talking to them as if they'd never been to the theater before. Rhoda rolled her eyes a bit but didn't say anything. The rest of the women were polite and listened.

"I know it might be hard to keep up with the story," Sabina said. "This is one of Secundus's most famous tragedies. Just remember that the men in white masks are playing the roles of the women, and the men in the brown masks are playing the roles of the men. The white costume means that one is supposed to be an old man, and the colorful costume means that one is supposed to be a young man. Yellow costume means a courtesan, short tunic means a slave. Um . . . purple costume is a rich person, red costume means a poor person. You'll get it as the play goes on."

The women followed the play well enough to be a little embarrassed by a few scenes. When it was over, they stood up and turned toward Sabina. "Now it's time for a pantomime," Sabina said.

"I want to see *Verae Matronae Romae*," Julia said excitedly.

"Are you sure?" Sabina said. "They're doing Catullus's *Laureolus* at the Theater of Marcellus."

Maria grimaced. "Oh . . . Catullus . . . I don't think that's a good one for us."

"All right, then," Sabina said with a smile. "*Verae Matronae* it is."

The women made their way to the Theater of Pompey, where the pantomime was already underway. A woman who was playing the part of Claudius's late third wife, Messalina, was dirty-dancing with a man playing the role of Silius, her lover, while another man playing the role of Claudius was limping and stumbling around the stage, seemingly oblivious to what was going on. The audience howled at Claudius's pratfalls and shouted, "Take it all off!" as Messalina and Silius groped each other. The woman playing Messalina was wearing a royal toga and crown, and was producing gift after gift out of the folds of the toga as the audience laughed. Finally she produced a long sword and started tiptoeing toward an unsuspecting Claudius. But a group of men playing Praetorian guards came from behind the scenery and mimed killing Silius, at which point Messalina turned the sword on herself and played out an extremely elongated death scene, to the cheers of the crowd. Everyone on stage then broke into a song. Sabina seemed to know the lyrics, but the other women could only make out the refrain:

Life is brutal, but at least it's short.

Maria wondered at the kind of life one would have to lead to have the free time to be able to learn the songs of the theater shows by heart.

"She didn't really kill herself," Sabina said to the other women. Maria was starting to feel as though they shouldn't be at the show, but the other women wanted to hear what Sabina had to say. "No, she didn't kill herself. Narcissus had her killed quietly without waiting for Claudius's permission. And then Claudius promoted him."

The second act began with another woman, very scantily clad, who was playing the part of Agrippina, Claudius's new wife. She chased the limping Claudius around the stage, and every time he fell, the audience laughed as she helped him up to resume the chase.

Rhoda leaned toward Sabina. "I heard she's his niece."

"That's right," Sabina said, waving a feather fan in front of her face. "He forced the senate to change the law forbidding marriage to a niece. But marrying a niece is better than marrying a whore like Messalina." She passed the fan down the row so the other women could take turns with it and get a break from the heat.

Prisca was shaking her head. "It's still incest. Nothing good can come of it."

Julia whispered, "The one I feel sorry for is young Brittanicus. His mother is dead, and now his stepmother has gotten her own son adopted by Claudius. That's not going to end well."

Maria frowned. "Ladies, let's not assume that all stepmothers are evil. Being a stepmother is a tough job. I can only imagine what it's like if your stepson is a prince."

Julia and Prisca gave Maria a knowing look of agreement. Sabina said, "Don't be fooled. The women have the real power. Agrippina rules Rome, make no mistake. She sits on a throne and rides around the city in a chariot, like a general or a priest. The men think they have it all worked out, with the laws in their favor, even giving them complete freedom to kill or have sex with whomever they want. But the women—we have our own forms of power, don't we? We control the dowries, and we have magic. We have spells and incantations, and if all else fails, we have potions. History may be the story of great men, but they are just marionettes on a stage. It's the women who hold the strings."

The other women looked at each other. All eyes landed on Maria. "Sabina," she said. "About the magic. The spells, the curses, the amulets." She gestured toward the medallion around Sabina's neck. "They don't really work, do they? I mean, you don't really believe they work?"

"Maybe they don't, but maybe they do," Sabina answered. "Anyway it's worth a try."

"I don't think so," Maria continued. "What I mean is, we believe that those things are, at best, a distraction from the real Deity. And at worst, they could bring evil spirits into your home."

"Really?" Sabina's eyes went wide. "You think that could happen?"

"Way-followers believe that putting your trust in magic is a kind of superstition. We put all that away like a girl puts away her dolls when she grows to be a woman. Astrology, too."

"Alright, now you've gone too far," Sabina scoffed, waving her hand in the air. "What could possibly be wrong with astrology?"

Someone in the crowd shouted, "Hey, Claudius! How about sending the *merda* carts around to clean up the streets?!" The audience burst into laughter.

Now the chase on the stage turned into a dance, with a steady stream of nude women dancing in from one side, looking at Claudius seductively and then miming their suicides as Agrippina handed them the sword, each in their turn. Then the woman playing Agrippina started stripping in front of Claudius, who mimed being embarrassed. The crowd went back to shouting, "Take it off!" and she didn't disappoint them. The play ended with the actors having sex on stage, and then a patriotic song, with the whole audience joining in. Julia was starting to look as though she felt sick, and Prisca was blushing and looking down at the floor. Maria and Rhoda realized it was time to leave, so they started getting up and ushered the other women out of the theater, making their goodbyes and thank-yous to Sabina as quickly as possible.

When Julia returned home to her apartment, Philologus and the children were not at home. She wondered where they could be but wasn't too worried about it until she heard a loud rumbling noise. Her heart skipped a beat. The loud rumbling turned into an even louder crashing, and Julia knew what was happening. A building was collapsing nearby. She couldn't tell how close it was, so she couldn't know whether the collapsing building was going to bring her building down with it. So she ran for the stairs.

Outside the noise was deafening. Everywhere people were running out of the buildings and into the street, pushing and shoving their way without even knowing which direction they should go. Julia called for her children. She spun around, looking in every direction, but she could not see them, and she could barely hear her own voice as she screamed their names until her throat was sore. The streets between the buildings were so narrow that not much light could find its way to the ground, and now a cloud of dust was rolling along the street, blocking out what little light there was in a gritty haze. Julia tried to figure out where the collapse was so she could run away from it, but she couldn't see farther than the length of one building, and she knew that if any of the walls around her fell she would be crushed. She could hear yelling and crying, and she strained her ears to see whether any of the voices belonged to her children.

Julia kept calling out her children's names even after her voice gave out. She ran to the end of the building and looked around the corner. People seemed to be running in the direction of the Forum of Augustus, so she ran that way too, hoping that her children were also running away from the collapse, praying that she would find them at the forum.

When the dust cleared, and her children were nowhere in sight, Julia ran back toward the collapsed building. She found it, now a pile of rubble, plaster, and wooden beams, and went to help pull the survivors out. All the while she kept scanning her surroundings, looking for her children. She was nearly blinded by her tears as she came upon the broken body of someone else's child, pulling the small, lifeless form from a heap of plaster and stone. Then she found another, and she was paralyzed. She desperately prayed to the Lord that her children were safe.

Julia worked as long as she could, digging through the rubble and helping to reunite other people's families. When her hands were raw and bloody, and the sounds of crying had dwindled, and when it was clear that there was no more she could do, Julia walked back to her apartment, hoping to find her husband and children at home. But she was disappointed. The apartment was empty. Not knowing what else to do, she started walking toward Stachys and Maria's house.

When Maria saw Julia covered in dust and dirt, with bloody hands, she ran to her and grabbed Julia's arms, looking into her expressionless face. "What happened? Where are the children?"

Julia tried to speak through her tears. "Building collapse. Not our building, another one. But I don't know where the children are. I was hoping they were here." Julia started to cry, and Maria pulled her close. Julia's head dropped onto Maria's shoulder, and her red ponytail bobbed up and down with her sobs.

"What's wrong?" It was Philologus coming in, covered in black dirt from head to toe.

Julia heard his voice and ran to him. "Oh, you're not hurt, are you? Were you buried in the collapse?"

"What collapse?

"An apartment near ours. Do you know where the children are?"

"Of course I do. They're at Pudens's house, with his daughters."

Julia breathed a sigh that immediately turned into crying. Through her sobs she asked, "Where were you? Why weren't they with you?"

Philologus smiled. "Because I got a job!"

"What?" Julia's tears were slowing, and her face started to light up.

"Yes, I got a job. It's dirty work, but the good news is the work won't be done for a very long time. I'm digging grave tunnels at the quarry. Senator Pudens, he gave me an old pickaxe and told me where they were digging, and I just showed up and signed on. I have a job!"

Marcus smiled. "Congratulations!"

Stachys seemed skeptical. "Wait. If you're digging grave tunnels, you'll be a social outcast, no better than a gladiator, a pimp, or an actor!"

Marcus jumped to Philologus's defense. "Stachys, old man, you're going to have to get used to the idea that Way-followers are already social outcasts. As long as we reject the traditions of Rome, we'll never be seen as good Romans."

"Yes," Philologus agreed, "and you heard Paul's letter to the Way-followers at Thessalonica. People are going to fall asleep. Way-followers, who will need a decent burial. Maybe I can help with that. We're going to need to take care of our dead as they wait for the resurrection. In fact, we could organize our gatherings as funeral clubs. That way everything would be legal."

Young Clemens joined the conversation. "He may be right. . . . Funeral clubs collect dues, so we can collect money to help take care of the widows and orphans. Funeral clubs allow both men and women, free and slave, and so do we. Funeral clubs have banquets, we have the *agapē* meal. It's perfect. Actually, it's kind of poetic. Our security is in the cemeteries."

"Well," Marcus said thoughtfully, "we can't make a decision on that until Peter arrives. For now, let's get ready for the gathering."

■   ■   ■

In another part of the city, in a butcher's apartment on Long Street in the valley between the Quirinal Hill and the Viminal Hill, another gathering of Way-followers was beginning their evening meal. The host greeted the group's leader. "*Salve*, Aquilinus!"

"*Salve*, brother. But I've told you—everyone calls me Linus."

"Linus, then. How is your father, old Herculanus?"

"He's well, thank you for asking."

"Ah! Ephebus. Linus, you remember Ephebus. He serves in the house of Narcissus. And this is Bito, from the imperial house."

"*Salvete*, brothers. Now, everyone! Everyone! Let's gather for the prayers."

After the prayers and petitions, Linus opened a scroll and read a story about a man named Daniel. He was thrown to the lions, but the one true God protected him, and the lions only licked his face, like harmless puppies. Then Linus set the scroll aside and said, "This story of Daniel happened a long time ago. But here we are in such an age that congratulates itself for being civilized, and yet people are still thrown to the lions. True, many of them are condemned criminals, but does that mean they cannot be saved? Iesua would say no, they can be saved. Iesua would say it's not too late for anyone to turn their lives around, turn over a new leaf, and start fresh. Brothers and sisters, I know that you gathered here are not likely to commit the kinds of crimes that would result in your execution. But I want you to consider whether you are participating in murder by going to the spectacles and witnessing, yes, even cheering, for the death of those men who end their lives in the arena. Some of them, their only crime was to be a slave and be unfortunate enough to be sold to the gladiator school. Here in the midst of these three days of games and shows, I believe that we Way-followers should not be attending them—even if we are ridiculed for avoiding the circus, the theater, the arena. Iesua himself said you are blessed when they ridicule you."

■ ■ ■

Peter looked up into the heavens and prayed. The small gathering of sailors and passengers lifted their eyes and their hands, and when Peter's prayer was done, they walked off singing, and the sailors headed back to their work, still singing the hymn. Peter's eyes scanned the horizon. He thanked his Lord Iesua, the one who was before Abraham was, for the colorful sunset that painted the sparkling water. But he could not see the coastline, and that worried him. He looked forward to reaching Ostia, where the ship would finally drop anchor. Peter thought about another time when he had longed to get to shore and drop anchor. It was the time a storm almost capsized his boat—that is, until Iesua calmed the sea. And now the Way-followers were tossed about on the rough waters of the empire. Peter thought about the anchor. He thought about how it could represent stability in times of tribulation and how it could stand for the peaceful, safe harbor of heaven. The Way-followers would need a symbol to unite them. Maybe the anchor could be such a symbol—standing for the stability of the faith and the hope of peace in eternity. Peter smiled. He could not think of a better symbol to represent the Way-followers and their good news.

■   ■   ■

The city was dark as a tomb but just as loud as if it were daytime. Stachys walked with his torch, dodging the carts and wagons, trying to stay out of sight of the night watchmen. The carts made an ear-splitting scraping sound as their iron-rimmed front wheels skidded on the paving stones to turn the corners. Mule drivers shouted at each other as the carts maneuvered past one another on the narrow roads. Porters unloaded their cargos, and the bakers began their nightly work. A large, loud group of people coming from a banquet sang their way down the street, surrounded by bodyguards with torches. Someone yelled about a cart wheel running over his foot. Stachys was startled when a group of people started banging pots and pans together to call the moon back to share its light.

Eventually Stachys found Urbanus by the warehouses. He started to say something to Urbanus, but Urbanus pulled him into an open warehouse stall and put his hand over Stachys's mouth. Urbanus crouched down and motioned for Stachys to do the same. There they waited.

Finally, Stachys whispered, "What are we waiting for?"

"You'll see. Now be quiet."

"Hades! It never fails. Always at the worst time, I have to go to the *forica*."

Figure 5.8. The Roman forica was the public latrine, which was equipped with a running water flush system. Since most people did not have bathrooms (beyond the chamber pot) in their homes, everyone expected to use the public facilities regularly.

Urbanus rolled his eyes. "Just hold it."

After a silence, Stachys whispered, "Urbanus, do you believe that there is one high god over all the other gods?

"I don't know. Some of the philosophers teach that there is. I suppose it makes more sense than all that rigmarole on the top of Mount Olympus. But how would I know?"

"The Way-followers believe in only one God. But it's not just a high god over the other gods. It's *only* one God. And the truly strange thing is, they say this God *loves* us. Isn't that weird? I know what love is between a man and his lover. But between a god and a man? They say this God cares what happens to us. Can you believe that? They say this God cares what happens to us, and then when we die, we go to paradise to be with this God."

"If that were true, then why don't they just kill themselves so they can get there sooner?"

Stachys stuck out his bottom lip. "That's a good question. I'll have to ask Marcus. They don't fear death, but they don't seek it either. And if one of them dies, the others are sad."

"The philosophers say that when you die, you come back and start all over again. That's probably what happens."

"You think?"

"Yeah. Trouble is, you can't remember the previous life, so you really do have to start over. You figure it out, or you don't. I guess the high god cares what you do, in the sense that he wants you to figure it out. But he doesn't go out of his way to help you. Then again, if Plato was right, why did they make Socrates kill himself? . . . Now, be quiet and wait. Soon you will be avenged for being mistreated. I want you to see this with your own eyes."

After a while they heard the brass nails of military boots coming along on the paving stones. Stachys was afraid it was one of the night watchmen. Urbanus made a sign for Stachys to be quiet. Then someone in the uniform of the Praetorians walked by the stall where Urbanus and Stachys were hiding. As he walked on, five gladiators stepped out from one of the other stalls and blocked his way. Stachys was shocked to see that the Praetorian was Geta, and then even more shocked when the group of gladiators started beating him with their fists and with clubs.

Urbanus defended his actions. "I hired the gladiators. Just to send the message to Geta that he can't threaten my freedman. I had to do something to answer the affront to my honor."

The gladiators finished their beating and ran off, leaving Geta lying motionless in the street. Urbanus waited for a short time, then stood up and slowly approached. Stachys followed but stayed behind Urbanus. Urbanus kicked Geta. "*Va cacá!*"

"What?"

"He's dead."

"No! Are you sure?"

"Yeah. I'm sure. Hades! They weren't supposed to kill him."

"What do we do?"

"Grab his legs."

"What?!"

"Get his legs. We have to get rid of the body before the night watchmen come along. You have to help me."

Stachys took Geta's legs, and Urbanus took his arms, and they dragged his body to the Tiber and rolled it into the churning water.

6

The Day of Saturn

Stachys did not go to Urbanus's house. He knew it was disrespectful to miss a morning visit to his patron's house, but given what had happened the night before, he was willing to risk Urbanus's anger in order to distance himself. And, he reasoned, a little prayer couldn't hurt, even if he had decided not to be baptized. So he went to the morning prayer gathering but kept to himself, avoiding conversation with Maria or Marcus. At several points during the meeting, Stachys closed his eyes and started to try to talk to the Lord Iesua, only to get distracted or find it difficult to put together the right words to express his fear and anxiety over his role in the death of Geta. Stachys desperately wanted to avoid any consequences, and in fact he couldn't even bring himself to think too much about what those consequences might be, let alone articulate them in prayer, but he remembered once hearing Marcus say that when you can't find the right words to pray, the Holy Spirit prays for you. At the time, Stachys had thought that was very strange, since Roman prayer depended on saying exactly the right words. How could the Way-followers pray without knowing the proper words? He didn't know how it could be true, but now he found he was counting on it.

Marcus ended the morning prayer gathering with a plea for his people to avoid the spectacles. "I know it's the third day of games, but we Way-followers should not be supporting the idolatry and brutality of the gladiator games and the shows in the theaters." He couldn't help glancing at his mother. "They turn humiliation and death into entertainment, and we can't be a part of that. Our commandments tell us not to bear false witness, which is what the plays do, and not to kill, which is what the games do. If we are not allowed to do something, we're also not allowed to watch it for entertainment. It makes us part of it. It makes us guilty of it." The people nodded their heads, but Marcus knew that some of them were planning to go to the games directly from the meeting. A few of them didn't even wait until they were out of sight of Stachys's house to look at their tokens and compare where they would be sitting in the amphitheater.

When Stachys told Maria what had happened during the night, she looked at him without saying anything for a long time. In her mind, she was a bit surprised at herself and how calm she was able to be, but then she had felt very distant from Stachys ever since the question of a tutor for Tertius had come up. Now as she looked at him, she could not remember why she ever thought it was a good idea to try to make a family with him. She shook her head and finally spoke. "I understand that *you* didn't kill this man and that you were put in a difficult position by your patron. But it's now clear to me that when the hard decisions come to you, you protect your career before you protect your family. Stachys, if you won't protect your son, I will. I'm sorry to say this, but if you hand your son over to a tutor, you and I are through."

"What?" Stachys didn't see that coming. By leaving him, Maria would be risking her very life. "You would sacrifice your own safety? You would be homeless, with no income. You would be putting yourself and Marcus in danger."

"Marcus is a grown man. As for me, I would rather risk my own security than stay with a man who would sell his son's innocence for a career advancement."

"But a woman on her own . . . I mean, if you had family here, or a dowry to get back, but you have nothing. No one. You would be opening yourself up to all kinds of dishonor."

Maria just folded her arms and looked away from Stachys.

"Maria," Stachys pleaded. "It's not that bad. It's just a difference in our customs, really. I mean, who are these Way-followers anyway, to tell us Romans what to do and how to live? What gives them the right to try to get me to live by their rules?"

"Some things are always wrong, Stachys. Always. Our rules are meant to protect the innocent. And it's not as though you and I have a registered marriage. I take my things, you keep your things, and we part ways. It's very simple. I promise it won't take too much time out of your day. Maybe our table isn't for you. Maybe you and I are not right for each other."

Once again Stachys found himself having to step out of his own house to find the space to think.

Most of Rome's elite would be at the Amphitheater of Statilius Taurus, on the south end of the Field of Mars at the bank of the River Tiber. Stachys decided to wander in that direction as he tried to figure out what to do next. But before he could come to any conclusions, he found himself at the amphitheater, and so he went in and found his way to a seat in the men's section. The sacrifices were just ending, and as wine offerings were poured out to honor Mars and Apollo, the wine dripped down the altar and soaked into the sand as a foreshadow of the blood that was about to flow there.

Maria left the house and found Tertius with his grammar school class. They were meeting in the street near the teacher's apartment. Maria apologized to the teacher, making excuses for

GLADIATORS AND THE ARENA

The English word *arena* is actually just the Latin word for "sand." It was in the sand that the gladiators fought and died. Although the earliest gladiator contests were in the open fora, by the time of our story, most of the fights took place in the amphitheaters.

An amphitheater was a theater in the round. Imagine two Roman theaters put together so that instead of a semicircle with the stage on the flat side, the amphitheater had an oval-shaped pit in the middle surrounded by stadium seating. The Amphitheater of Statilius Taurus may have been the only true amphitheater in Rome at the time of our story, though we don't know exactly where it was. However, it's important to keep in mind that gladiator contests were also held in fora, in circuses, and possibly also in theaters. The Colosseum was not built yet—it would not be built for another thirty years.

Like the other spectacles, the gladiatorial games always began with some form of pagan ritual. And like the theater, an amphitheater had separate seating for men and women. There was also a section for schoolboys, with their tutors nearby to watch over them.

A typical day at the amphitheater might begin with public executions. If one went to the arena in the morning, one might expect to see criminals who were sentenced to die *ad bestias*, that is, by the wild beasts. Other executions were conducted by making two condemned criminals fight to the death. In the afternoon the professional gladiators would be paired off and fight.

Most gladiators were slaves, bought by the trainers as an investment and then trained to fight. Some volunteered for various reasons. They got a signing bonus, which may have been the incentive if the person was in debt. There were even a few female gladiators. It seems that there were enough gladiators that most of them only actually fought a few times per year. Of the ones who died, most died in their first or second fight, but if they survived to the third fight, odds were better that they would survive for some time. If a gladiator lived and fought honorably for three years and then put in another two years of service as a trainer, they earned their freedom. Gladiators could rent themselves out as hired security guards on the side, and with the prize money from their victories they could buy their freedom. Some became quite rich and famous, with their portraits and busts on display in the homes, shops, taverns, and bathhouses of their fans.

We should keep in mind that not all fights ended in the death of the loser. If the gladiators were slaves, they were considered valuable property, in whom a significant investment had been made in terms of training and food. Even if the gladiator was not a slave, trainers were acting as booking agents, and so it was in their best interest to make matches that resulted in both gladiators surviving. Owners were not in a hurry to lose that investment just because their man lost a match—especially if they had money on the match and lost that as well. In any case, there was such a thing as an honorable defeat, and if the crowd—and ultimately the emperor, if he was in attendance—felt that the loser's life should be spared, then he would have lived to fight another day. The truth is, many of the matches were probably more like a form of sparring than a fight to the death. The gladiators probably did try to draw blood, but they probably also tried to avoid mortal wounds.

Early Christian writers generally denounced the gladiator shows as barbaric and as participation in murder. However, the urgency with which they begged their flock to stop going to the shows tells us that they were in fact having a hard time getting the Christians to stop attending. There were a few more philosophically minded pagans who also recognized that the gladiatorial games were detrimental to civilized society. The Stoic philosopher Seneca wrote against the games in his *Moral Epistles*, but then he was exiled by the emperor Claudius.

Figure 6.1. Painting of a Roman arena with gladiators (National Archaeological Museum, Naples)

Tertius, and then took him from the class. She was determined to protect him, even if it was not her legal right to do so. She took him to Senator Pudens's house, where she planned to ask whether Tertius could spend the day with Pudens's daughters, away from the games and out of harm's way. When she arrived at Pudens's house and was shown into the atrium, she found Marcus there, along with young Clemens. They were talking with the senator about the plan for smuggling Peter into the city.

"I'm sorry to interrupt," Maria said. "I was hoping that Tertius could stay here for a while."

"Mother, what's wrong?" It was clear she was upset.

"We'll talk about that later," she answered. "I just need a safe place for Tertius right now."

Senator Pudens said, "Of course he can stay here." He motioned for a slave standing by to come closer. "Bring my daughters." The slave nodded and left the atrium. Soon Pudenziana and Prassede came in, followed by Scrap. The children bowed to Maria.

Maria turned to Tertius. "Tertius, you know the senator's daughters. And of course you know Scrap. You can stay with them for the day. Now, why don't you go play some games." She gave Tertius a little shove in the direction of the girls. Tertius didn't say anything but did as he was told and followed the other three children as they walked out of the atrium.

Pudenziana tried to find something to say to break the ice with Tertius. "Scrap," she said, "tell us the story of your name."

"You've heard it a thousand times," he protested.

"But Tertius hasn't, have you, Tertius?"

"Not from Scrap himself," Tertius said.

"Go ahead and tell it!" Prassede started the pleading, and the others joined in until Scrap relented.

"All right, all right. My name is Scrap because on the day I was born, I was left on the garbage pile in one of the alleys of the Suburra. The midwife, I suppose, left me there to be exposed because I was unwanted. I was like garbage to my own mother and father. But I wasn't about to just lay there and die. I cried! I cried and I cried, and I yelled and I screamed. And someone heard me." The sisters clapped their hands. Scrap smiled and continued. "It was my master's son, young Clemens. He was passing through the Suburra, and he heard me crying. So he came to the garbage pile to see what all the noise was. And when he saw that it was an abandoned baby, well, he couldn't just walk away. Because even though he was only twelve years old, he was a Way-follower, and he had heard Peter say that every person is made in the image of the one true God. Every person is loved by our Lord. So he picked me up from the garbage pile and took me home. His father, who is not a Way-follower, decided to call me Scrap. But someday, when I am free, I will take my master's name, and I too will be called Clemens."

Pudenziana and Prassede clapped their hands, and Tertius smiled to hear details of the story that were new to him. "I was fortunate," Scrap concluded. "Many babies die on the garbage pile because there are not enough Way-followers to pick them all up."

At that same hour, another baby was fortunate. Lucius Geta's body was found in the marshy area along the river south of Marble Street, near the Fish Market. Word of Geta's death came to his household just before his wife gave birth to a baby girl. His orders to drown her were never carried out.

■ ■ ■

Stachys looked around the amphitheater. Women of the senatorial class wore their finest and most colorful tunics and shawls, each trying to outdo the next with their clothing and jewelry. For the wealthiest of Romans, this was the place to be seen. The plebeian women were in their section, up at the top of the bleachers, most of them hardly paying attention to the action in the arena. Stachys noticed the boys' section, with their tutors seated nearby. They looked so young. He looked back and forth between the boys and their tutors. He tried not to think about what it was like when he was that age. He tried hard not to think about it, but in trying not to think about it, all he could do was think about it.

Then Stachys knew what he had to do. He had to protect his son. He had to do what his own father could not do for him, because he had been a slave. But Stachys was free. He had to say no to Urbanus. That was going to be hard.

Stachys wondered at the words he would use as the first animal hunts of the day began. Slaves brought in scenery backdrops, large plants, and other obstacles for the animals to hide behind. Stachys allowed himself the luxury of postponing his dilemma for a short time as he watched the hunters taunt a bear with nets and spears.

As the morning wore on, the shows moved from people hunting animals to animals hunting people. Convicted criminals were sentenced to die by the beasts, and so one by one, condemned men were sent out into the arena to face the lions, tigers, bulls, and boars. The emperor Claudius and his wife Agrippina appeared, to a mixture of cheers and boos from the crowd. They sat in the imperial ringside box, between the priests and the Vestal Virgins. Claudius seemed to be in a good mood. Agrippina fanned herself and looked bored.

When the excitement of the emperor's arrival died down, Stachys decided it was time to find Urbanus and give him the news—though he was dreading the conversation, it wouldn't be wise to put it off any longer. He got up from his seat and started moving down toward the section where he knew many of the equestrian businessmen sat. He scanned the crowd as he walked. Eventually he saw Urbanus sitting by himself in a less crowded section. Many people were going out to get lunch as the "noontime gladiators" were starting. The first pair of condemned criminals fought to the death, and when one of them died, another came out to fight the winner. This went on for some time as Stachys sat next to Urbanus in silence, pretending not to notice the stares of Urbanus's fellow equestrians, who recognized that Stachys was seated above his social class. Neither one of them said anything until the last round was complete, one condemned criminal lived to fight another day, and the musical interlude started.

Urbanus was the first to speak. "You didn't come see me this morning."

"I'm sorry. I meant no disrespect," Stachys said.

"I know. I'm not upset with you. I understand. It was unfortunate, what happened last night. But as long as we keep it to ourselves, we should be fine."

"And the gladiators? Will they keep quiet?"

Urbanus paused, then said, "If they are not fortunate today, then we are fortunate."

"We can't simply hope they all die in the arena."

"That's why we're here, isn't it?"

Stachys knew the time had come to tell Urbanus. "I have to tell you something."

Urbanus sighed.

"I'm sorry, but I have to say no to you. I won't be hiring a tutor for my son."

For a moment, Urbanus looked indignant, yet it seemed that he could not find the words to respond to Stachys. He was saved by a loud musical fanfare. So he just stared at Stachys, fuming in silence.

Now the professional gladiators came out into the arena. Slaves, criminals of lesser offenses sentenced to the gladiator schools, even a few volunteers who signed up as a last resort to get themselves out of debt all marched around the arena, presenting their arms to the emperor. Behind them marched twelve of Claudius's freedmen carrying the fasces, the bundled axe and rods that symbolized Rome's power of corporal and capital punishment. The freedmen bowed to Claudius, lowering the fasces in deference to his imperial power. The gladiators bowed and saluted.

THE FASCES, S. P. Q. R., AND IMPERIAL POWER

The fasces are the bundled rods and axe that symbolize Rome's power of corporal and capital punishment. By the time of our story, they had come to symbolize the personal power of the emperor. Our English words *fascist* and *fascism* come from this concept. Whenever the emperor walked in a procession or parade, he was followed by men carrying the fasces to remind the people that his power was absolute.

The acronym S. P. Q. R. stands for *Senatus Popolusque Romanus*— "the Senate and the Roman People" (the *Q* comes from the suffix -*que*, which was one way to say "and" in Latin). During the time of the Roman Republic, this acronym was meant to convey the idea that the Senate and the people ruled together. Back then the people had a voice in their government through voting. But in the empire, the people had lost most of their voting rights, and the acronym was little more than symbolic.

Because Julius Caesar had been assassinated by the senators, the first true emperor, Augustus, distrusted the Senate and made the Praetorian Guard his personal bodyguard, something like our Secret Service. When Caligula was assassinated, the Senate debated trying to restore the republic—in other words, many hoped they could go back to not having an emperor. But in reality that could never happen, because the Praetorians were too powerful, and they had proclaimed Claudius the new emperor. So the transition from republic to empire was in a way the transition from "the Senate and the Roman People" to "the Senate and the Emperor." Caligula had switched the balance of power to "the Emperor and the Senate," and with the reign of Claudius the Senate lost much of its power altogether—with Claudius elevating freedmen to positions of authority and inflating the senate class with new foreign families—so that the real rule was in "the Emperor and the Praetorian Guard."

Figure 6.2. An example of the acronym SPQR on a statue base. Capitoline Hill, Rome.

Claudius stood and shouted to the gladiators, "Be brave, men. Die well, if today is your day to die. Do not run from your opponent so that your death takes place on the edge of the arena where only a few can see it. Confront your opponents in the center of the arena, where all may see your bravery, either in victory or in death." Then the emperor saluted, and trumpeters played a fanfare as the first of the gladiators took up their positions.

"How can you say no to me?" Urbanus said, clearly exasperated. "I'm your patron. Is it because of this Chrestus, your other lord?"

"No. Or at least, not directly. Let's just say that I must say no to you because my father was not able to say no to your father."

"You regret being my father's favorite boy?"

"Urbanus, did you have a tutor when you were Tertius's age?"

"Yes."

"Do you wish your father had said no?"

Urbanus didn't answer. After a long pause, he said, "It doesn't matter. I didn't get the position, so you, or rather, your son, is no longer relevant."

Stachys should have been relieved, but he wasn't. The death of Geta was weighing heavily on his mind.

He and Urbanus allowed the cheering of the crowd to be a welcome distraction from their conversation. The first gladiator had fallen. His opponent stood over him with his sword at his throat and looked to the crowd. The people cheered, booed, and many made the sign of thumbs up or thumbs down, depending on whether they thought the defeated man had fought bravely and deserved to live to fight another day. The victorious gladiator looked to the emperor's box. Claudius stood, and the crowd grew silent. Claudius turned his thumb upward, to indicate that the winner should take the coup de grâce and kill the defeated man. Stachys and Urbanus watched in silence as the victor thrust his sword into his opponent's jugular notch. Then he stepped away from the dying man as a slave dressed as Charon, the ferryman of the river Styx, came out and broke the defeated gladiator's skull with a sledgehammer. The body was then dragged away, and the sand was groomed for the next match. The Praetorians shooed away the potion dealers who tried in vain to get some of the sand soaked with gladiator's blood.

Stachys stood up to leave. Urbanus looked at him, seemingly with surprise, but didn't say anything. As Stachys walked toward the exit, four Praetorians walked in, pushing their way through the crowd.

It didn't occur to Stachys that they were coming for him until it was too late. But even when they grabbed him, he thought they were just going to throw him out for sitting in the wrong section. Urbanus turned to run in the other direction but ran into another group of Praetorians.

Eight Praetorians in all dragged Stachys and Urbanus out of the amphitheater as their most important business associates looked on in shock and horror. Once outside the bleachers, in the amphitheater's arched stairwell, the Praetorians tied their hands behind their backs. Stachys was panicking, pulling at the ropes around his wrists, remembering the threats of torture at the Praetorian barracks. Urbanus was shouting to the soldiers, "Do you know who I am? Do you know who my patron is?!" The Praetorians just laughed and shoved the two men out the gate and into the street. The soldiers walked Stachys and Urbanus along, pulling and shoving, causing them to trip, and then smacking them when they fell. Stachys's knees buckled out of fear, and he could hardly support his own weight. In his mind he was frantic with the realization that his only hope for justice was also tied up right next to him. Urbanus was wild with anger and denial, and he kept shouting, "No! No! Stop! Wait!" But the soldiers shoved them on.

They moved southeast along the river, enduring the stares of the crowds in the street and the sting of the Praetorians' rods and fists. Turning east toward the Fontinalis Gate, Stachys could see his home in the distance. His body instinctively turned toward home, but a soldier kicked him in the direction of the gate and the Capitoline Hill.

The climb up the hill seemed like a long, painful eternity. As they finally reached the top, the Praetorians shoved Stachys and Urbanus east toward the Tarpeian Rock, a cliff overlooking the Old Forum. Narcissus was waiting for them there.

The Praetorians stood Stachys and Urbanus at the edge of the cliff. Narcissus spoke to them, not looking at them but looking out over the Old Forum.

"Urbanus, I'm surprised to see you here, in the middle of all this. But I have the testimony of four gladiators, swearing that you hired them to attack Geta."

Urbanus tried to think fast. "The testimony of gladiators is not admissible in court."

Narcissus's tone turned to one of contempt. "Look around you— are we in a court? Urbanus, I tried to help you. I tried to gain a very respectable—and lucrative—position for you. And how do you repay me? By speaking nonsense in the presence of the emperor. You made me look like a fool, and so I have no regrets about your fate." Narcissus looked Stachys up and down. "And who is this?"

Urbanus answered, "My freedman, Stachys. The oil merchant, and a Way-follower." Stachys turned to look at Urbanus with a horrified look on his face.

Narcissus raised an eyebrow. "What is a Way-follower?"

All eyes were on Stachys. He cleared his throat. Did he dare contradict his patron? That could make things worse. He cleared his throat again.

"Well?" Narcissus was getting impatient.

"I am in the school of the Way-followers, which is to say I am not initiated to their table—yet."

"That does not answer the question." Narcissus pushed Stachys even closer to the edge of the cliff. Stachys's foot slipped, and he had to lean backward to avoid going over the edge.

"Um." Stachys's mind raced. "Way-followers are like Judeans in their prayers, in their belief in one God, in their burial of the dead, and in their modesty about their bodies. But they are not like Judeans in some ways. They do not refrain from certain kinds of foods, and they do not require men to cut their . . ."

"Enough!" Narcissus was unable to conceal his impatience. "Did I ask to join their school? No! I simply asked what a Way-follower is."

Stachys thought about the Way-followers he knew. In a flash, all of the people he cared about went through his mind. Tertius, Maria, Marcus, the people who gathered in his home for prayer. Even annoying old Ampliatus. Then his mind came to rest on Scrap, and a newfound courage filled his heart. "A Way-follower," he said with his head held high, "is someone who cannot hear the cry of a baby from the garbage pile and just walk away."

Narcissus was quiet for a moment. Then he said, "So are you one of these Way-followers, or are you not?"

Stachys hesitated, but only for a moment. "I am."

Narcissus turned his gaze back out over the cliff. "Do you know," he said thoughtfully, "that in the days of the republic, traitors were executed by being thrown off this cliff?"

Urbanus and Stachys remained silent.

Narcissus continued to speak as he looked out over the Old Forum. "In many ways, this rock is Rome. It represents the power of Rome to destroy whatever threatens Rome's traditions. Your feet feel as though they are on solid ground. But one little shove, and you would fall to your death. So what is to stop me from throwing you both from this rock right now?"

Urbanus said, "My freedman and I are both citizens."

"Ah yes, citizens. Entitled to a trial, and to a quick and painless execution. You will have both." Narcissus turned and walked away.

The Praetorians pulled Stachys and Urbanus from the edge of the cliff and pushed them in the direction Narcissus was walking, across the Capitoline Hill and down into the Old Forum. At the edge of the Old Forum, the Praetorians walked Stachys and Urbanus to the dungeon known as the Tullianum, an underground prison created by the previous emperor, Caligula, especially for political prisoners. Stachys was suddenly filled with regret for all his doubts and silently prayed to Iesua, begging him to save

ROMAN CITIZENSHIP

Most people who have read the New Testament are aware that the apostle Paul had Roman citizenship, which (at that time) meant that he had certain rights and privileges, including that he could not be executed without a trial in Rome. We don't know how Paul got citizenship, or why, but normally Roman citizenship was reserved for natives of Italy. For those from the provinces it could be given as a reward for services rendered to the state, or in some cases it apparently could be bought with a bribe. Although we do not read in the New Testament that Paul was ever asked to provide proof of his citizenship, he must have had a bronze "diploma," inscribed with the grant of citizenship for his family. At the time of our story, we know that the emperor Claudius gave them out as a reward for loyalty.

There were two different levels of Roman citizenship. Full citizenship included both private and public rights. All Italians would have had the private rights, allowing them to conduct business and make a contract (including a registered marriage). Technically women still needed a guardian to make a contract, though a woman who had three or more children (four or more if a freedwoman) could make a contract on her own.

In addition to the private rights, landowners also had public rights, which meant that they could hold political office. Foreigners living in Rome had none of the rights of citizenship, which means that at this time most Christians were probably not citizens.

The freedmen of citizens received citizenship (private rights) upon manumission, and their children were considered free citizens, even if they were non-Italian. Therefore, slavery could actually be an avenue to citizenship and social mobility that was not available to the free poor. Roman law was written to protect citizens, especially those with public rights (landowners).

them. The Praetorians replaced the ropes around Urbanus and Stachys's wrists with iron shackles and put their feet in irons. Then Stachys and Urbanus were lowered into the dungeon.

. . .

When Sabina heard that her husband had been arrested, she tried to find out where they were holding him, but no one would help her. Even some of her friends, the wives of senators, refused to receive her in their homes. Sabina felt betrayed by her own social class. Then she remembered Prisca. Another noble lady, but a Way-follower. Not knowing what else to do, Sabina made her way to Prisca's awning shop. Her heart sank when she saw the store-front closed, with the boards across the front and the door locked.

A familiar voice came from behind her. "Hello, Sabina." Sabina turned. The voice belonged to Sabina's newest Way-follower friend, the elderly Susannah.

"Susannah, I'm relieved to see you. I was hoping to find Prisca."

"Ah. She's at Maria's house. I'm on my way there now. Everyone is meeting to pray for Stachys and your husband."

Sabina could not help being struck by the contrast between her friends' response to her situation and the response of the Way-follower women. "Really? They're praying for my husband? I don't understand. They hardly know us, but they're willing to be associated with us, even now? I'm grateful for that, because my friends have abandoned me. I want to go with you, but first let me go to the magic dealer and buy some curse tablets."

Susannah smiled. "My dear, I'm glad to see that you are disillusioned with Roman high society. But a curse is not our way. It's easy to hate, I know. But what you really need is to pray and hope."

"Hope." Sabina sighed. "Hope is yesterday's venison. Only one day away from being spoiled. No, I must *do* something," Sabina choked on her words as she fought the urge to break down.

"Prayer *is* doing something," Susannah said. "Come. Let's go to the prayer meeting."

.   .   .

Julia kept interrupting Marcus's prayers with the sounds of unsuccessfully trying to hold back her sobs. She and Maria held each other as Marcus led the desperate prayer.

Prisca wiped her eyes. "We were at the theater yesterday. They sang this song, it was something like, 'Life is brutal, but at least it's short.' How do we live like this?"

Marcus tried to answer the question. "Prisca, we have to focus on our hope—the hope of eternal life. Peace comes from keeping our minds focused on that. Eternal life is bigger than this life."

Maria started to cry openly. She was worried that if Stachys died before being baptized, he would not be able to look forward to eternal life. She tried to dry her tears and change the subject. "Where's Rhoda?" No one seemed to know. "Johnny . . . I mean, Marcus . . . tell us a story about Iesua—something that will give us hope."

"Mother, you knew him better than I did. I was too young to be a disciple."

"Tell them about the time you were praying in the garden with the disciples."

"No, Mother, no one wants to hear that story."

"Come on, it will make everyone smile."

"It's not a funny story. It was the night Iesua was arrested."

"Please tell it," Prisca said softly.

Marcus could not resist Prisca. "All right," he sighed. "When the soldiers came to arrest Iesua, everyone was running in all directions. We were all afraid, even the older men. Only Peter stood his ground and drew his sword. Took a swing at one of the soldiers, too, but the soldier ducked it and the sword hit this poor slave named Malchus, who was holding a torch for the high priest. Took his ear right off. But Iesua healed it." Marcus stopped as though the story were finished.

"Come on, there's more to the story!" Rhoda was coming in the door with a smirk on her face.

Marcus sighed again. "So anyway, when we were all running in every direction, trying to get away from the soldiers, one of them grabbed for me. Now, what you have to understand is that it was really hot out that night, so I had taken my tunic off and was wearing just my loincloth. And wouldn't you know, the soldier grabbed the loincloth, and it came undone. And I was naked. And I ran all the way home naked."

The group laughed a little, still wiping tears from their eyes. "You must include that in your biography," Prisca said.

"I don't think so."

■　■　■

Urbanus and Stachys had no idea how long they had been in the dungeon when the silence of the prison was broken by the sound of young girls' voices. Stachys lifted his head to listen. He knew those voices. It was Pudenziana and Prassede, talking to the prison guards.

"We've brought food and water for the prisoners," Prassede said.

"And this basket is for you," Pudenziana added, showing the guards that her basket held a pile of bronze *sesterces*. "You'll treat them well, won't you?" The guards nodded as they opened the hatch that led down from the street into the dungeon. A basket of food and a jug of strong wine were lowered down for Stachys and Urbanus.

"How did you know?" Stachys asked the girls.

Pudenziana distracted the guards while Prassede whispered. "Slaves from Narcissus's house. They came and told us. Your wives are beside themselves." Prassede went on to inform the men what else Narcissus's slaves had overheard. Stachys and Urbanus were to be marched outside the wall and beheaded in just a few hours.

Stachys buried his face in his hands, but Urbanus reacted with anger. "No trial?"

"The emperor is still at the amphitheater. Narcissus means to do this without his knowledge, to appease the Praetorians."

"Girls!" Stachys said urgently. "Forget about us. It's not safe for you to be here. Prassede, where is your sister? You can't trust these guards."

"Don't worry," Prassede answered. "We've bribed them to treat you well. As far as they know, you could be here a long time, so they're hoping the bribes will keep coming. And anyway, young Clemens and some of the others are watching from a distance. So we're safe. But we should go. We're all having prayer at Marcus's house."

As the girls left, Stachys mumbled, "It's actually my house. *My* house." He shook his head.

Urbanus seemed surprised. "I can't believe your friends came here. I can't believe they're not worried about being caught and sentenced along with us. I'm grateful for the food, but obviously we won't be here long enough to starve to death."

"There is hope for us, Urbanus."

"What hope?"

"The Way-followers are praying for us. That means something."

"But they're only praying to one god? Shouldn't we be praying to as many gods as possible?"

"You can pray to whatever gods you choose," Stachys said with determination. "But in my experience, the gods of Greece and Rome have never proven themselves to me. This one God of the

Way-followers is different. If you had seen the things I've seen, and heard the stories I've heard . . . I'm going to pray to the Lord Iesua. Either he will save me or I will die. But I'm certain that without him on my side, I will die."

Both men were quiet for a while. Stachys prayed silently—his lips moving but making no sound. Eventually Urbanus said, "It's not just me. If I die, I die. But Sabina will be disgraced. And my daughters will be ruined. Will they be reduced to prostitution? The gods know they can't sing, so they won't be actresses. What will be left for them if I'm gone? I can't imagine . . . and to think I almost exposed one of my girls."

Stachys was thinking of his own family. "Maria, and my stepson Marcus—they're not citizens, and Marcus is a Judean living in Rome illegally. If they're connected to me, they'll be crucified. And Tertius, who will protect him? I thought I could give them security by advancing my career. You were right, Urbanus, advancement is dangerous. It just brings you to the attention of those who stand to lose when you gain. I can't give them security. Now all I can do is entrust them to the Lord and to the fellowship."

Urbanus said, "Stachys, you seem to have an advantage over me."

"How's that?"

"You have this extended family who, even though they're not related to you, will risk their own honor for you. It's as though they want to be associated with you at the very time when you're at your least honorable."

"That's the time when I need them the most."

"Who are these people?"

"The Way-followers. The church."

"What is the church?"

"It's a little like a military cohort—loyal to each other and to our Lord, no matter what. Even in the face of death. Because life is bigger than death. Bigger than this life. The church is the cohort

Figure 6.3. The main Roman road from the city into Ostia

of people who have received mercy from the Lord Iesua. And the cohort is growing. Soon it will be a legion."

"I wish I had a chance to become part of a cohort like that," Urbanus said. "Hmm. Bigger than life, eh? Do you suppose that if we promise to be devoted to your God, he will save us?"

"I only know that the one true God can't be bribed. But it never hurts to ask. I've heard of the Lord Iesua helping people escape from prison. It's strange to think that I was considering suicide, but now that I might die, I don't want to. Now I want to live. Doesn't matter, though. Even if we escaped, what would we do? We can't live as outlaws, always looking over our shoulder. How could we ever have any peace?"

A few hours later, Narcissus and his Praetorian guards returned, pulled Urbanus and Stachys out of the dungeon, and started the procession to the place of execution. Stachys's wrists were bruised, and every shove from the soldiers sent shocks of pain up his arms. Urbanus shuffled along, his eyes glazed over, a blank expression on his face. From the Tullianum the procession turned eastward on the Sacred Way, heading through the Old Forum toward the Capena Gate and the Appian Way.

As the group crossed the Old Forum, a gang of men shouting slogans for the green team came out of nowhere and stood in the middle of the path. Another group was waiting for their cue behind the altar of the deified Julius Caesar, and with a nod from Rhoda, they jumped into the mob shouting slogans for the blue team, and a brawl ensued. The Sacred Way was blocked. The Praetorians turned

Figure 6.4. Remains of the Temple of Vesta (heavily restored)

south toward the other side of the Old Forum, and then turned east again, which brought them right past the house of the Vestals.

As the procession went by the temple of Vesta, the Vestal Virgins filed out of their gardens and onto the street, again blocking the path of the execution procession. Narcissus was

Figure 6.5. Remains of the garden of the House of the Vestals

visibly agitated, but there was nothing he could do. He could only watch as Julia stepped up and whispered into Claudia's ear, then Claudia whispered into Vibidia's ear.

As everyone stood still and watched in silence, Vibidia moved regally, walking slowly up to the soldiers. The only sound now was the rustling of her vestal robes. She stood face to face with Narcissus and looked him square in the eyes. Narcissus met her gaze, but the other soldiers bowed their heads in reverence and looked at their boots. Vibidia cleared her throat as everyone waited for her to speak. "On the authority of the Pontifex Maximus, and by the intervention of the goddess Vesta, these men are pardoned. You are to release them immediately."

Narcissus ground his teeth. The law was on her side. There was nothing he could do. He glared at Claudia and vowed to himself that someone would pay for this—maybe not today, but someday.

Soon both Stachys and Urbanus were back in the arms of their wives.

■   ■   ■

As Marcus prepared for the evening meal and worship, Stachys and Maria tried to talk privately, but it was an awkward mix of expressions of relief and mundane platitudes. Although Stachys knew Maria was genuinely happy that he was safe and at home, he could tell she still felt a bit distant.

"Don't worry," he said. "Tertius will not have a tutor." Maria let out a sigh that almost turned into tears. She buried her head in Stachys's chest, grabbed onto his tunic, and pulled him close to her. He put his arms around her. "Anyway," he continued, "Urbanus didn't get the job as prefect of the grain supply. But you were right, Maria. You were right. Thank you for being a mother to my son." Now Maria started to cry into Stachys's tunic. "It's going to be all right. We're all safe now."

As the gathering was beginning, there was a knock at the door. Prisca opened it and welcomed Urbanus and Sabina into the room, with their two daughters. Sabina noticed the humble status of most of the people at the gathering. She bowed to all of them and said, "Thank you for your hospitality."

Marcus responded with a smile. "We were all once wanderers and strangers to the truth. But Truth herself has given us hospitality and made us citizens of her own city, so now wherever we go we are her ambassadors."

The door swung open again. It was one of the slaves of the house of Aristobulus. He came in just far enough to say, "It's time. He's here."

Marcus nodded to Stachys. "Are you up to this?"

"Yes, I'm ready," Stachys said with conviction.

"Good, then go now—find Clemens and tell him it's time."

The slave was still standing in the doorway. "There's a problem. One of our friends said Peter's name out loud and someone heard it. We're not sure, but they may have recognized him. Our friends have him hidden for now, but it's not going to be easy to get him out of Ostia and into the city."

"All right," Marcus said. "Go with Stachys, and when you find Clemens, make sure he understands the situation." Stachys nodded, and he and the slave left. Marcus turned to Urbanus. "Urbanus, I hate to ask, but did you come in a litter?"

"Yes."

"Can we borrow it?"

"Of course."

"Thank you. Philologus, Ampliatus, go with Urbanus's litter bearers, and take them to Ostia. Along the way, I want you to talk to the empty litter as if there is a noble lady inside. If anyone says anything to you, tell them to get out of the way and make way for the noble Sabina."

Some hours later, the litter bearers, led by Philologus and Ampliatus, arrived in Ostia at the Seven Sages Tavern. Philologus and Ampliatus went in, trying to look inconspicuous as they scanned the main room. Merchants drinking, sailors singing and playing drinking games, a row of small tables at the back where men played and bet on illegal backgammon games. Then they spotted Bito, one of the Way-followers from the imperial household, who was sitting alone in the corner. He pointed out the men who had recognized Peter. They had heard someone say his name when he first came in, and now they were sitting at a table, waiting to catch another glimpse of him. But Peter was nowhere in sight.

"Where is he?" Philologus asked.

Bito answered with a smile and a shake of his head. "He's in one of the hourly rooms, telling a prostitute about Iesua."

Then young Clemens burst through the tavern door with a group of men, singing and stumbling, pretending to be drunk. Clemens pointed to Ampliatus and shouted, "Peter, my friend! It is so good to see you! We've come to see you off to Greece! Come! We will take you to your ship and say our goodbyes there."

The men who had heard Peter's name earlier looked confused and started second-guessing themselves. So when Clemens's gang surrounded Ampliatus and took him out of the tavern, they followed the group. They followed them down a dark narrow street, taking the long way toward the harbor and away from the tavern.

Peter cautiously emerged from a back room. Philologus looked at him with admiration. There he was—the apostle. Full face. Strong jaw. With a full head of curly white hair and a white beard. Peter smiled and hugged Philologus as they kissed each other's cheeks.

They left the tavern, and when no one was looking, Peter got into the litter. Philologus and the litter bearers made their way back to the road that led to Rome, and Clemens and his gang circled back to follow at a distance and make sure they were safe. By morning, the whole group was back in the city, and Peter was in Rome.

As dawn approached, a group of Way-followers was waiting near the pyramid-shaped mausoleum of Gaius Cestius. The group was ecstatic to see Peter again, though they tried to be quiet and keep a low profile. Peter got out of the litter to walk the rest of the way, and Urbanus's litter bearers took their leave. Philologus led the joyful group through the Raudusculan Gate, in the direction of Pudens's house. But as they made their way around the curved end of the Circus Maximus, they were stopped by a group of retired gladiators, hired muscle for Claudius's freedmen.

"What's this?" One of the gladiators looked Peter up and down. Philologus scanned the group. He could see Narcissus's men standing behind the gladiators. He looked around for a way out.

One of Narcissus's men said, "We heard there were some Judeans trying to sneak into the city. I think these must be them, no?"

The leader of the gladiators put his hand on his sword. "Must be."

7

THE DAY OF THE SUN

BEFORE THE GLADIATOR COULD draw his sword, a large hand slapped down onto his wrist and gripped it tightly. The gladiator winced in pain as the meaty hand squeezed. The hand had a tattoo on it—four letters across the four fingers of the fist: S. P. Q. R. It was the hand of a centurion.

The centurion said, "These aren't the ones you're looking for. Now move along, barleymen."

The gladiators looked at the centurion. Then they looked at the squad of soldiers behind him. Then they took their hands off their swords and walked away.

The centurion walked up to Peter. He stared at Peter, then he smiled.

Peter smiled and said, "Cornelius!" The two men gave each other a bear hug and kissed each other's cheeks. "Cornelius, my friend, I didn't know you were in Rome!"

"I just dropped anchor. Pudens said there might be trouble. Allow me to escort you."

Peter looked at Cornelius's hands. "I see the legionary tattoo. But what's that on your other hand? V. P. M. S. What does that stand for?"

Cornelius smiled. "It stands for *Vade Post Me Satana*."

Peter shook his head. "'Get behind me, Satan.' Thanks for the reminder of Iesua's rebuke."

"Relax, Peter," Cornelius said, as he started walking in the direction of Pudens's house. "It's not personal. It wasn't really about you then, and it's not about you now. Just a little reminder to myself that the real battle is not against flesh and blood. But I'm impressed you were able to translate that so quickly. Your Latin is pretty good."

"Ever since Pentecost."

The morning prayer gathering at Pudens's house was buzzing with excitement, and it was difficult to keep everyone quiet. Many Way-followers from the other gatherings had come to Pudens's house, and the presence of both Peter and Cornelius was making it hard to get everyone to settle down.

Peter finally got their attention and said, "Everyone, I want to introduce you to a friend of ours, Cornelius. He is one of the first non-Judeans to become a believer, so he knows what it's like for most of you, who have been grafted onto the family tree, so to speak. Cornelius, this is Anacletus. He's our leader this morning."

Cletus shook Cornelius's hand. "Call me Cletus. Peter, are you sure you don't want to lead?"

"No, just pretend I'm not here."

Cletus smiled. "I'm sure that's not possible."

After the prayer meeting, the shepherds of all four gatherings met with Peter, along with the other leaders of the Way-followers in Rome. Marcus, Linus, Cletus, and Apelles were there, as were the deacons Philologus, Ampliatus, and young Clemens, as well as Julia and Prisca. Peter gathered them close. Scrap hid behind a curtain to hear what Peter was saying.

"Brothers and sisters, it's good to be back in Rome. Thank you

EVANGELIZATION AND CONVERSION IN THE EARLY CHURCH

The early church was not a "seeker sensitive" kind of experience. Especially during times of persecution, early Christians might have been suspicious of anyone who walked in off the street claiming to want to join. In fact, it's hard to imagine anyone asking to join the church without first knowing church members intimately.

Conversion in the early church was through relationships. We have to remember that in the Greco-Roman world, people didn't generally think of themselves as individuals the way we do today. And for those of us who live in the United States, with concepts such as personal freedom, human rights, and the possibility that one person can "make a difference" in the world, it may be hard for us to understand that none of those things would have seemed possible for anyone but the "one percent." The Roman personality was formed as part of a group, and so a Roman person's identity was not as an individual but as a member of a group—usually a family, but then also as a part of other connections, including patron-client networks, trade guilds, sports-team factions, and, yes, religious cults. This means that conversion into a religious movement was generally not an individual decision—or if it was the decision of the head of a household, it affected the whole household.

Add to this the fact that for Christianity, a decision to join also meant a commitment to abandon all Greco-Roman religious loyalties, and we can see that almost no one would have joined the church without bringing a support system along. This means that in the early years of Christianity, most of the conversions were conversions of families, who were then drawn into the larger family of the church. The church became their

---

new extended family—often replacing the actual extended family that may have ostracized them.

For more information on the growth of Christianity in the early centuries, read the works of Rodney Stark, especially *The Rise of Christianity* (Princeton University Press, 1996) and *Cities of God* (HarperOne, 2007).

---

for watching over the flock while I was away. I bring good news from Jerusalem and the other apostles."

"Only good news?" Philologus seemed worried.

"Yes, Philologus, only good news. Why? Does my arrival come with a dark cloud?" And then the smile left Peter's face as he remembered the first time he arrived in Rome, coming with the news of the death of James. "Oh, right. Well, thank the Lord, nothing like that. Now I know you've heard about the council, but there's something I didn't say in my letter. I wanted to tell you in person."

The group was silent, ears at attention.

"We have agreed that from now on we are to call ourselves . . . Christians."

Everyone spoke at once. "Not Way-followers?" "What does it mean?" "What is a Christian?"

Prisca said, "I understand. Christians. Because we are followers, not only of the *way* of the Lord, but we are followers of the Lord himself. He *is* the way. *Christian* means followers of the *Christos*."

"Yes, but it means more than that," Peter said excitedly. "Remember that *Christos* means 'one who is anointed.' So just as Iesua is *the* Anointed One, the Messiah, we as Christians are also anointed by God and adopted as God's sons and daughters."

More chatter from the group. "Christians." "We're Christians."

Peter continued, "We now have four thriving gatherings in Rome, each with over fifteen baptized believers at the table. And someday, when Judeans are allowed to come back to Rome, the gathering at Prisca's shop will make five. And we're growing. That means it's no longer going to be practical for the deacons to be runners, taking the Thanksgiving Bread from one gathering to the rest. So I'm giving all of the shepherds—Marcus, Linus, Cletus, and Apelles—the authority to preside over the prayers that consecrate the Thanksgiving Bread. So then each gathering will have its own presider, who will function as the *paterfamilias* of that group of Christians. He will watch over his flock, and he will say the prayers over the bread and wine. The deacons—Philologus, young Clemens, Ampliatus—you men will assist in the serving. You will still take the Thanksgiving Bread out to any who are sick or who cannot be at the gathering, and you will care for the sick and let the shepherds know who is in need. And if a woman is sick, and there is no man in her house to chaperone, then the women will go out and care for her. Susannah will be a guide for the women, and I need you ladies also to keep your ears open to any who might be in need and let the shepherds know. If our Lord brings to our attention anyone who is sick or starving—if we can help them, we should. Even if they're not Christians. And if any of our number should die, Philologus will be in charge of the burials."

Marcus spoke up. "But you will be here, too, Peter. Right?"

"I will, Marcus," Peter answered. "I'll stay in Rome as long as I can, and I'll share the ministry in Pudens's house, since his gathering is the largest." Peter paused in thought for a moment. "I remember one of the last conversations I had with our Lord. He asked me whether I loved him. And then he told me to take care of his sheep. So, just as Iesua is the Good Shepherd over us all, the flock of each gathering of the church needs a shepherd.

Just as God is our Father, each gathering needs a housefather. We need this structure for several reasons. We need it so that every baptized believer will have access to the sacred mystery of the Thanksgiving Bread. And we need it so that we can make sure that the teachings Iesua gave us are faithfully and truthfully handed down from one generation to the next. And finally, we need it so that we will be able to take care of those who are sick or hungry or imprisoned."

Marcus asked, "Is Paul coming to Rome?"

"Not anytime soon," Peter answered. "He's concentrating on going to places where there are no Christians yet, where people don't know about Iesua. And, to his credit, he said he didn't want to step on my toes by coming to Rome and trying to build on the foundation I've laid. He'll come eventually, I'm sure. He wants to go to Spain, so he's going to have to come through Rome at some point."

When the meeting broke up, Peter took Stachys aside. He put his hand on Stachys's shoulder and gripped it as he looked Stachys in the eyes. "Stachys, I'll get right to the point. We're going to need another deacon. Marcus says you're ready for baptism, so are you up for it?"

Stachys was stunned for a moment. "I'm sorry, Peter." Stachys shook his head. "Marcus has no idea. He means well, but I am *not* ready for baptism. You don't know what I've been through."

"I heard a little about it. But it sounds like you've turned a corner with your faith. From what I hear, it sounds like you're ready to make the commitment to live as a Christian."

Stachys couldn't look Peter in the eye. "It's not that. I can make that commitment now. But you don't know . . . what I did. What I said."

"Sit down here." Peter gestured toward a bench. Stachys sat down on the bench, and Peter sat next to him. Stachys thought that Peter was sitting a little too close for comfort. Peter leaned in toward Stachys and whispered, "Tell me."

Stachys didn't feel ready to talk about it. But deep down he knew he needed to tell someone. "The first time . . . when they asked if I was a Way-follower . . . I said no. I denied being part of the family, so how can I ask to be initiated to the family's table?"

Peter smiled. "Oh, Stachys. You couldn't know this, but I once asked the same question." Peter's tone of voice changed as his eyes suddenly became red and watery. "Even though I walked with him on the water . . . briefly. Even though I had all the proof I should need for my faith to be solid as a rock, I still denied him. Not once but three times. At the very time when Iesua needed friends the most, I said I was not his friend. Stachys, I know what it's like to be afraid. And I know what it's like to act out of fear and say and do things that later made me ashamed and horrified to think that it was I who did and said those things. But Iesua forgave me. He had compassion on my weakness. And look at me now, sailing all over the empire as his ambassador. If I can be an apostle, surely you can be a deacon."

"But do you really want me? There must be others more qualified."

"Stachys, sometimes the ones who needed the most forgiveness are the ones who are the most grateful and become the most enthusiastic ambassadors of our Lord. And I'll tell you something else. Before his ascension he gave me and the other apostles the authority to forgive sins in his name—to go and find his lost lambs and bring them back to the flock. So in the name of Iesua, I release you from your sin, freeing you to serve him. And I seal you with the sign of his passion, the once-and-for-all sacrifice for the forgiveness of all who claim him as their Lord." Peter used his thumb to trace a small cross on Stachys's forehead. "And as soon as you are baptized, you will be one of the deacons of the church at Rome."

■ ■ ■

In the afternoon, all of the Christians of Rome gathered at the River Tiber, just south of the cattle market, near the Greek Quarter. The sun was bright but not hot. The breeze was cool and healing. Peter waded into the shallow part of the river near the bank and motioned for the catechumens to follow him. Stachys, dressed in a new white tunic, was the first to move down into the water. He was followed by a few families with their children and several others. Stachys was suddenly hit by the gravity of what was about to take place, and he felt like he needed more time to prepare for it, so he stepped aside to let the others go first.

When it was finally his turn, Stachys walked up to Peter, the cold waters of the Tiber swirling past his thighs. He bowed his head, and Peter put one hand on Stachys's head and the other on his shoulder. "Stachys," Peter began, "Do you believe in the one true God, and no others?"

"I do."

"Do you believe that there is no salvation but through his unique Son, Iesua the *Christos*, and that there is no other name under heaven by which we may hope to be saved?"

"I do."

"Do you believe that he conquered death by dying and inaugurated the resurrection by rising from death?"

"I do."

Peter gently pushed Stachys down into a kneeling position. The cold water was now up to Stachys's shoulders. "Stachys, I baptize you in the name of the Father . . . and of the Son . . . and of the Holy Spirit . . . as our Lord Iesua commanded us to do." With each of the names of the persons of the Trinity, Peter pushed Stachys's head underwater, then pulled him up again by the back of his tunic. Maria was smiling so hard her face was starting to hurt. But she didn't care. This was the day she had been waiting for.

Then Peter put both of his hands on Stachys's shoulders. "Stachys, receive the Holy Spirit."

When the baptisms were done, and all of the newly baptized Christians were confirmed in the faith with the gift of the Holy Spirit, Peter addressed the group. He could see a small crowd gathering behind the Christians as onlookers stopped to see what they were doing. He recognized this as a chance to plant the seeds of faith in whoever might be listening.

"Brothers and sisters," he shouted. "The one true God sent his Son into the world to offer forgiveness and reconciliation. All he asks is that you turn to him in faith and remain faithful to him alone. When you do this, and are initiated to his table in the way we have done here today, you receive two gifts: forgiveness of your sins and the indwelling of the Holy Spirit. These gifts will lead you to salvation and eternal life. This is the promise that the one true God has made to you, and to your children."

As Peter led the newly baptized Christians out of the river, the first to congratulate Stachys was Ampliatus. He grabbed Stachys's hand and shook it vigorously. "Welcome to the Lord's table . . . brother."

Stachys sighed and smiled. He returned the handshake. "Thank you . . . brother."

"Pardon me," Maria said with a tear in her eye. "May I give my husband a kiss?"

. . .

For the rest of the day, Peter visited all four of the active home gatherings, talking to as many of the people as possible and asking everyone to spread the word that the evening *agapē* meal and worship would be for all of the Christians of Rome, all together at the house of Senator Pudens. While he was at Stachys and Maria's house he blessed the unions of Stachys and Maria and of Philologus and Julia.

Sabina watched the couples as Peter blessed them. She squeezed Urbanus's arm. When it was over she whispered to him, "I want that. I want that kind of marriage. Not a contract, but that . . . what did he call it? One flesh. Where I have only you, and you have only me. And we don't have to worry that one of us is going to leave if a better match comes along. Is there any way we could have that?"

Urbanus turned to face his wife. "My dear, you're the one who married beneath your status. If anyone were going to worry, it would be me. But the truth is, I don't think we're going to have any choice in the matter. That's the kind of union that's expected of these Way-followers. It will be expected of us . . . when we join them."

∎ ∎ ∎

That evening, Pudens's atrium was overflowing with joyful people, all excited to have Peter among them again. They milled around as Peter walked through the group greeting old friends and meeting new ones. Urbanus and Sabina arrived with their daughters, Tryphaena and Tryphosa. After a while Pudens called everyone together and welcomed them to his home, and then led the group into his private auditorium, where he often read to his household or sponsored lectures. The walls were painted with colorful and elaborate patterns of garlands and geometric designs. An expensive-looking chair with a back on it was placed at the front of the room on a platform, with a curtain behind it. The men gathered on the left side of the room, and the women and children on the right.

Peter deferred to Linus, who led the opening prayer. After the prayer, Maria chanted, "Lord, have mercy," and the whole group echoed back the words.

Then Peter nodded to Marcus, who took up his scroll and began to open it. Marcus said, "I'm so glad our brother Peter is back in Rome. As you know, I've been working on writing the story of the time when Iesua was with his disciples. I call it *The Memoirs of Peter*. But I can't finish it without more help from the man himself."

Peter interrupted him. "Brother Marcus, please don't call it *The Memoirs of Peter*. My name should not be in the title. It's not really about me. I hope you're including as many of the stories about Iesua as you can, so if anything, it's the memoirs of all the apostles."

Marcus nodded humbly and began to read:

Iesua took Peter, James, and John and led them up a high mountain apart by themselves. And he was transfigured before them, and his clothes became dazzling white, such as no fuller on earth could bleach them. Then Elijah appeared to them, along with Moses, and they were talking with Iesua. Then Peter said to Iesua, "Teacher, it is good that we are here. We will make three tents: one for you, one for Moses, and one for Elijah." He didn't know what he was saying because they were so terrified. Then a cloud came, and overshadowed them. Then a voice came from the cloud, saying, "This is my beloved Son, listen to him."

The people gathered were amazed at the story, and after a brief silence, they began asking Peter to tell them what it was like to be there. Peter sat down in the chair at the front of the room. He smiled and said, "This is another reason why your memoir should not be named after me. I just don't come out looking all that good in these stories. Oh well, the Lord wants me to stay humble, I suppose. What was it like to be there? To be honest, I almost wasn't there. I was so scared I almost ran away."

Peter was lost in thought for a brief time. "I was with Iesua and the Zebedee brothers. We were on the holy mountain, and our Lord willed that we should see the majesty of his resurrection body. Looking back on it now, he looked very much the same as he did after his resurrection, when it was hard to recognize him. But that time, the light of his glory was so bright I fell in a faint, and my eyes were blinded. I remember seeing nothing, but hearing his voice as he was talking with Moses and Elijah—though I couldn't hear what they were saying. When I could see again, well, I can't even describe it to you. I'll tell you, that thing I said about building three tents? I was just trying to get Iesua's attention so he would remember we were there and not burn us to a crisp with his glory. I didn't know what I was saying. But I'm glad I didn't run away, because if I had, I might not have heard the Voice. You know, many people started to follow Iesua, but a lot of them didn't last. They left him. Yes, it's true. But I could never leave him, in part because I heard the Voice."

Peter thought for a time and then went on. "All of us here, we all came from different places. It seems as though so many people in Rome are from somewhere else. Judea, Phrygia, Cappadocia, Egypt—even Asia. Some of you were there at Pentecost. A few of us knew Iesua personally. But it doesn't matter where we come from or who we were before. Because now we are Christians. Now we are the church. I heard Paul say something at the council. He said no matter whether we are Judean or not, slave or free, man or woman, we are all one in our Lord Iesua, the *Christos*. In fact, we all come to him like the thief on the other cross, trying to have faith, hoping he will give us that peace that comes from the hope of paradise."

A voice from the back of the room shouted, "When will Iesua come back? It's been almost twenty years!"

Peter smiled. "It isn't for us to know times or seasons. But the fact that he has delayed his return is an act of mercy. He's waiting for as many people as possible to come to reconciliation with God through him. Also, since he seems to be delaying his return, it's good that Marcus is writing down the story, for as you know, some Christians have already died, and more may die, and we may even find ourselves with second- and third-generation Christians—our descendants who will have to hand the faith on to people who never met anyone who walked with Iesua. But don't worry, a thousand years are like a day to God. So any delay does nothing to diminish the promise."

"So where was I?" Peter continued. "Yes, the hope of paradise. The transfiguration and resurrection of our Lord show us that we are not to believe the fables of an afterlife as a shadowy existence, as the myths of Hades and Elysium claim. And we are not to believe in the afterlife as a disembodied existence, as the philosophers teach. No, we believe in the resurrection, which even King David prophesied in the psalm that begins, *Keep me safe, O God, in you I take refuge.* The philosophers, in fact, can't even agree on what it means to be blessed. The Pythagoreans say reason is the key to the good life. The Sophists claim individualism and relativism. Socrates said it was law, and Plato said it was justice. The Skeptics say the best thing you can do is admit you don't know. The Cynics prefer detachment, and the Epicureans pursue pleasure. The Stoics claim to have defined virtue, but look around you—are the Romans virtuous? Are they happy? No, Iesua said that the ones who are blessed are the poor, and those who mourn, and the humble, and the hungry. Those who show mercy, and those who make peace. The pure . . . and the persecuted."

Marcus muttered to himself, "I should be writing this down."

Peter continued, "But why should those people be happy or feel blessed? Because they know they will inherit the resurrection life in God's eternal empire. They put their hope in something bigger than life."

Cletus led the prayers, which went on for quite a long time with such a large group. But eventually the prayers came to a conclusion, and Pudenziana and Prassede brought the bread and wine forward and placed them on a small table in front of Peter. Peter nodded to Rhoda, who led the gathering in the singing of a text from the prophet Isaiah:

Holy, Holy, Holy, is the Lord of hosts.

All the earth is filled with his glory!

Holy, Holy, Holy, is the Lord God Almighty,

Who was, and is, and is to come!

Peter led the group in the Our Father, and then they all prepared to receive the Thanksgiving Bread by reciting a prayer of confession from the Psalms:

Be gracious to me, O God, according to your mercy. According to the greatness of your compassion, blot out my transgressions. Wash me thoroughly from my iniquity, and cleanse me from my sin. For I know my transgressions, and my sin is ever before me. Against you, and you alone, I have sinned and done what is evil in your sight. . . . Create in me a clean heart, O God, and renew a steadfast spirit within me. Do not cast me away from your presence, and do not take your Holy Spirit from me. . . .

After Peter said the prayers over the bread and the cup, he held them up for all to see. He raised his voice and said, "I heard Iesua say, *Whoever eats my flesh and drinks my blood has eternal life, and I will raise him up on the last day. For my flesh is true food, and my blood is true drink. Whoever eats my flesh and drinks my blood lives in me, and I in him. As the living Father sent me, and I live because of the Father, so whoever eats me, will also live because of me. This is the bread which came down out of heaven; not as the ancestors ate and died; but whoever eats this bread will live forever.*

"Later, Iesua would say, *Take this, all of you, and eat it: this is my body which will be given up for you. Take this, all of you, and drink from it: this is the cup of my blood, the blood of the new and everlasting covenant. It will be shed for you and for all so that sins may be forgiven. Do this in memory of me.* Look—here is the Lamb of God, who takes away the sin of the world." Peter broke the bread, and all the baptized solemnly came forward to receive it from him.

When Stachys received the bread, he held it in his hand and looked at it. He hesitated, letting the gravity of the moment sink into his mind. He remembered some words of Iesua that he had heard. *Remain in me, and I will remain in you.* He ate the bread, and a sense of peace washed over him, and he thought he was beginning to understand what they meant when they wished each other the peace of the *Christos*. When the wine was passed to him, he tried to take a small sip. He tried to be unselfish and make sure he wasn't taking too much. But he wanted the blood of the *Christos*, and he couldn't help himself. He took a big gulp and smiled.

After all of the baptized had received the body and blood, Peter addressed the gathering. "I would like to say a few things before we sing our song. First of all, I've asked one of our newest initiates to join the order of deacons. Brother Stachys has accepted the responsibility of service." Everyone expressed their approval and wished blessings on Stachys as he blushed. "And finally, we will be taking a collection for the poor brothers and sisters of Rome. Many of us here are unemployed, or have not had enough work recently, and are struggling to survive." Now it was Philologus and Julia who blushed. Peter smiled at them and continued, "Those who have some resources to spare are asked to share what they have. Brother Stachys, in his first official act as a deacon, will be going around the room with a basket. Please be generous."

Maria and Rhoda led the hymn together. The people all knew the song because they had been singing it in their individual gatherings for a while, but this was the first time that all the Christians of Rome sang it together.

Let all creation wait in silence, as we praise the Father, Son, and Spirit

Let all creation say Amen, as we praise the source of all our blessings

WORSHIP IN EARLY HOUSE CHURCHES

Just as conversion in the early church was not simply an individual's decision, the group mentality of the Roman personality meant that worship also was not simply a matter of personal devotion. Most early Christians did not think in terms of personal Scripture study or personal prayer and meditation. For early Christians, worship was more about celebrating the group identity as people who gathered at the table of the Lord and who collectively identified with Jesus Christ as their Savior. The idea of a "personal" Savior would probably not have made much sense to them.

We don't actually know much about what music and singing was like in the early decades of Christianity. There may have been varying "degrees" of what might be called hymnody, on a spectrum going from rhythmic speaking, to intoned speaking, to chanting, to melodic singing. The songs included in our story are based on the theory that the apostle Paul quoted hymns in his letters. However, there is a lot of debate among scholars about whether the quoted passages are in fact hymns or perhaps prayers. In any case, if Paul is quoting preexisting material, then the content of these songs or prayers is very significant, since it represents the earliest Christian theological statements we have in written form. For more on these pre-Pauline hymns, see my book *Trinity 101* (Liguori, 2012).

When we ask what early Christian music may have sounded like, the question becomes even more complicated. No doubt the music of the first Christians was not very different from the music of ancient Jews, but in a place like Rome, it also must have been influenced by Greek and Roman forms of music. We know for sure that they did sing, and Paul encourages his people to sing "psalms and hymns and spiritual songs" (Eph 5:19; Col 3:16; see also 1 Cor 14:15, 26). Unfortunately, we don't know how Paul defined these three types of songs or whether they were really three different things at all.

Singing in the first churches was probably responsorial, that is, a call and response, with a leader singing a line and the people repeating it. Or perhaps a soloist sang a phrase, and the people responded by singing "Amen." Eventually the congregations would have memorized longer passages, possibly set to music, and sung them in unison. But even if the songs were set to music, they did not have harmony the way modern music does, with different singers singing different notes based on chords. As far as we know, all singing in the church was in unison until the Middle Ages.

We also don't know for sure whether they used musical instruments at all. If the heavenly worship scenes in the book of Revelation are a reflection of actual worship, then the early Christians may have used lyres (usually translated "harps"). They may also have used pan pipes. However, even then the music was not so much an accompaniment as it was a guide for the singers. The instrument would simply play the melody as the people sang along. In later centuries we know that many musical instruments (horns, drums, cymbals) were probably avoided by the church due to their association with pagan worship or erotic dance. Note that the instrument often translated "flute" was not actually a flute but was a reed instrument called an *aulos*, something like an oboe or clarinet.

The song in the story near the end of this chapter is a simplified version of an early Christian song known as the Oxyrhynchus hymn. This was a third-century hymn with music notation found on a papyrus in the city of Oxyrhynchus. The version I've adapted is a much-simplified, modernized arrangement, but the English words do convey the theme of the Greek

Figure 7.1. Modernized version of the Oxyrhynchus hymn (third century), adapted and arranged by the author

text, and the tune is based on melodic phrases from the music. I've also added modern chords so that I can use it as a worship chorus with my students. I hope you will try it yourself and sense a connection with those who worshiped in the early centuries of our faith.

As the people talked and sang their way out of the gathering, Stachys went around with the basket collecting donations. When he came to Urbanus and Sabina, they stopped him. Urbanus said, "Stachys, my friend. We've told your man Peter that we want to join the school of the Christians, both of us, and our daughters. It may ruin our reputation, but then I'm not sure we will have much of a reputation left after all that's happened."

Sabina smirked. "Of course, *my* reputation was ruined when I married *him*."

Urbanus sighed, smiled, and put his arm around Sabina. "My wife's vocation is to ensure my humility. In any case, Peter said that we would need sponsors—to vouch for us when we're ready to take up the lifestyle. The irony here is not lost on me, but I'm asking you, will you and Maria be our sponsors?"

Stachys smiled. "Of course, my friend. Nothing would make us happier. And soon we will call each other brothers."

Urbanus pulled out his small leather pouch and fished out his most prized possession—the rare gold coin. He rubbed it for luck, then dropped it in the basket.

MAP OF FIRST-CENTURY ROME

N

VATICAN HILL

XIV
Trans Tiberim

JANICULUM

PINCIO

Flaminian Road

P

VII
Via Lata

CAMPUS
MARTIUS

T

M

L

IX
Circus
Flaminius

XIV
Trans Tiberim

H

CAPITOLINE
HILL

E

C

A
VIII
Forum
Romanum

B

N

IV
Templum
Pacis

S

12

11

10

QUIRINAL
HILL

VI
Alta Semita

G

O

VIMINAL
HILL

F

K

2

1

16

15

14

13

3

Tiburtinian Road

III
Isis et
Serapis

V
Esquiliae

ESQUILINE
HILL

V
Esquiliae

COELIUS

II
Caelimontium

4

5

6

7

I
Porta
Capena

D

X
Palatium

PALATINE
HILL

XI
Circus
Maximus

I

XIII
Aventinus

AVENTINE
HILL

9

8

Ostian Way

R

XIII
Aventinus

Emporium

Testaccio

XII
Piscana
Publica

Q

Appian Way

0m 200 400 600 800 1km

1 Porta Collina
2 Porta Viminalis
3 Porta Esquilina
4 Porta Querquetulana
5 Porta Caelimontana
6 Porta Capena
7 Porta Naevia
8 Porta Raudusculana
9 Porta Lavernalis
10 Porta Trigemina
11 Porta Flumentana
12 Porta Carmentalis
13 Porta Fontinalis
14 Porta Sanqualis
15 Porta Salutaris
16 Porta Quirinalis

A Old Forum
B Forum of Augustus
C Forum of Caesar
D Urbanus' House
E Stachys' House
F Pudens' House
G Butcher's Apartment
H Apelles' Apartment
I Prisca's Awning Shop
J Palatine Hill/Claudius' Palace

K Praetorian Barracks
L Theater of Pompey
M Field of Mars
N The Suburra
O Tiburtinian Road
P Flaminian Road
Q Appian Way
R Ostian Way
S Cattle Market
T Saepta Julia

OTHER BOOKS
BY JAMES L. PAPANDREA

From Star Wars to Superman: Christ Figures in Science Fiction and Superhero Films

The Earliest Christologies: Five Images of Christ in the Post-Apostolic Age

Handed Down: The Catholic Faith of the Early Christians

How Christianity Saved Civilization: And Must Do So Again (with Mike Aquilina)

Rome: A Pilgrim's Guide to the Eternal City

Trinity 101: Father, Son, Holy Spirit

Reading the Early Church Fathers

The Wedding of the Lamb: A Historical Approach to the Book of Revelation

Novatian of Rome and the Culmination of Pre-Nicene Orthodoxy

Spiritual Blueprint: How We Live, Work, Love, Play, and Pray

The Adventures of the Space Boys: The Space Boys Meet the Moon Bully (illustrated by Joe Groshek)

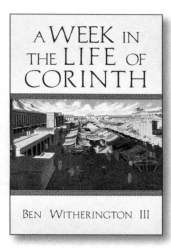
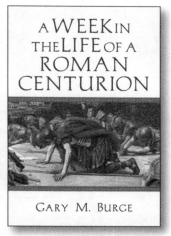
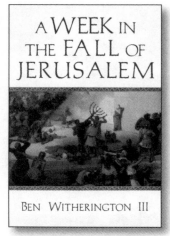
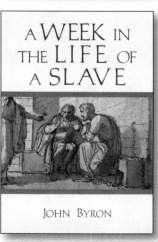

Finding the Textbook You Need

The IVP Academic Textbook Selector
is an online tool for instantly finding the IVP books
suitable for over 250 courses across 24 disciplines.

---

ivpacademic.com